Undeniable Bond

The Bonded Series, Volume 2

Reese Spenser

Published by Happy Endings Publishing, 2020.

This is a work of fiction. Similarities to real people, places, or events are entirely coincidental.

UNDENIABLE BOND

First edition. March 31, 2020.

ISBN: 978-1393329985

Written by Reese Spenser.

Chapter 1
Avery

IT HAS BEEN THREE WEEKS since the sharks smelled blood in the water. One of which Lucian and I spent at his beach house in East Hampton. He worked from home mostly, driving back to Manhattan twice, and returning to me each night by dinnertime. Lucian surprised me one sunny afternoon by taking me to the Montauk Lighthouse. He couldn't have picked a more gorgeous day to visit. The lighthouse was beautiful and tranquil, and the robin's egg blue sky was perfect. We walked the path to the water, climbing down the rocks to the beach. The waves were a little rough, but it was wonderful. We took the stairs to the tower. The climb is not for the faint of heart, as the steps are narrow and curvy, but it's worth the climb to see the sunset and the magnificent view of the Atlantic Ocean. At the top, we enjoyed a glass of wine, while sitting on a blanket, eating from our picnic basket. The lookout was breathtaking: the cliffs, the ocean and a killer sunset. It was a great outing, made even more spectacular by the three earth-shattering orgasms Lucian gave me.

We're back in Manhattan now, and I've moved in with Lucian. He's kept his promise, finding out who was responsible for leaking the lies to the tabloids about me. The perpetrator confessed to breaking into my apartment. He claims he wanted to prove there was more to my story. The damage, however, has already been done. Avery West will forever be linked to Marisa Hunter because there was some truth to the story.

Stretching in bed, my muscles ache deliciously. An involuntary tremor causes my center to clench. I remember how Lucian made love to me so tenderly last night, and then fucked me into oblivion. Since confessing our love, we can't seem to keep our hands off each other. We make love every night, sometimes all night. His energy is endless, and the control he has over his body is a major turn-on. Holding back his own release, until he has made me come at least twice. His sexual appetite consumes me, leaving me sated and overwhelmed at the same time.

I know he's feeling guilty for the role Philip played in my tainted past. There is no way I could ever blame Lucian for anything his biological father did to me. Philip Hunter abandoned both his children. First, Lucian, when he was just a baby. Although Philip giving up his rights to be a parent to Lucian, was the best thing that could have happened to him. Philip was abusive to Lucian's mother, nearly beating her unconscious the night she found out she was pregnant. Then, there's me. Philip married my mother and adopted me, and for a little while we were a happy family. That all changed when my mom died. I was fifteen when Philip revealed his true self to me. A gambler, an alcoholic, and a man who willingly prostituted his daughter and sold her virginity to settle a debt. I'll never forget any of the horrific things that happened to me. However, I choose not to live in the past. I choose not to let those tainted memories haunt me or define my future with Lucian.

Shaking off the ghosts of the past, I climb out of bed. Padding barefoot across the floor I make my way to the bathroom. I brush my teeth and pee before taking a shower.

Twenty minutes later, I'm feeling refreshed and ready to start the day. I follow the aroma of fresh coffee brewing, down the hall to the kitchen. Lucian has set the timer on the coffee maker for me. I smile, wondering how he knew what time I would get out of bed. It still feels strange being in the penthouse without him. Although I've come to consider the penthouse as my home, I sometimes miss my apartment in Chelsea. I've decided to rent it out for now, putting most of my personal items into storage.

Lucian's spare bedroom has become my new home office, giving me a place of my own to work. With my things from my home office of the Chelsea apartment, the space feels familiar. He refuses to let up on the security detail, insisting that once we became a couple, a bodyguard was inevitable.

Opening the fridge, I take out Greek yogurt and mixed berries. I put the Greek yogurt and mixed berries in the bowl along with some homemade granola. Taking a seat at the breakfast bar, I gaze out the large window. Enjoying the view of the New York City skyline, I almost miss the sound of my phone ringing.

Hurrying to the bedroom, I grab my iPhone from the bedside table.

Breathless, I answer.

"Hello."

"Well hello to you too gorgeous." Wyatt's husky tone comes through the line.

"Hey, Wyatt." My own voice is clearer now. "What's up?"

"I was hoping you're free for that lunch you promised." The line is quiet for a long moment. "I just want to catch up. It's been awhile, and I've missed my friend."

"What did you have in mind?'

"You. Me. And lunch at my place, say around one."

"Wyatt." His name rolls off my tongue in exasperation.

"I promise to be on my best behavior," he soothes, hearing the irritation in my voice. "We're friends, I get it. You're with Thorne. Message received loud and clear."

"Alright, your place at one."

"I'll see you then." I can hear the smile in his voice.

We end the call and I hurry back to the kitchen to finish my breakfast.

Over breakfast I call William, informing him of my lunch plans. William Mathers is a quiet man, not at all intrusive. There are times when his presence is barely noticeable, which is quite a feat considering his stature, standing well over six feet three inches. I know this because he's slightly taller than Lucian. His muscular frame is impressive, and his features are hardened, like a man who has experienced the pain of loss. His buzz cut and straight posture tells me of his military experience while his deep soulful brown eyes speak of his heartbreak. He has only been my bodyguard for a couple of weeks since Lucian and I got back from the Hamptons. The first day with him chauffeuring me around town while I ran errands, was a little disconcerting. I didn't like the idea of arriving everywhere in a limousine. I thought it brought more attention to me. Attention I didn't want. Lucian remedied that three days later. William now drives a fully customized BMW 760i sedan, a gift to me from Lucian. I don't think the man has any idea what tone it down means. The car is beautiful. The luxurious leather seats and footrests makes commuting around the city heavenly. The built-in Wi-Fi allows me to work while I'm on the go. It seems he's thought of everything, including the two ten-inch entertainment screens. A luxury I never knew I wanted, until I had it.

I busy myself for the next few hours, researching my next article. With the manuscript done and safely in Marcus's possession. I can work on a few other projects. The thing I love most about freelancing is that I can work when I want. Having a flexible schedule has always been a major selling point... that and being able to choose my assignments.

Closing my MacBook, I check the time. Realizing I've worked longer than intended, I rush to the bedroom to change into something suitable for lunch. The T-shirt and leggings I'm currently wearing isn't something I wear in public. I'm dressed and ready when I hear the doorbell. Grabbing my iPhone and purse, I leave the bedroom.

William is waiting for me in the foyer. He greets me cordially as I approach.

"Good afternoon, Miss West." His tone is professional, yet friendly.

"Good afternoon, William." It doesn't matter how many times I tell him to call me Avery. He insists on addressing me formally. "I'm ready," I say summoning the elevator.

The door to the elevator opens. I step inside, and William follows. We ride down to the garage in comfortable silence. When the elevator comes to a stop on the garage level the door slides open and William steps out first. He surveys the area before indicating all clear. I know these precautions are for my safety, but sometimes it's ridiculous. There has been no other incident after the break-in and the leak to the press.

Once we reach the BMW, William opens the door for me. Climbing inside, I settle into the luxurious leather seat, making myself comfortable. William shuts the back-passenger door, rounds the front of the vehicle, and takes his seat behind the wheel.

We travel to Park Avenue, the Prestons' brownstone where Wyatt occupies the smallest apartment, on the first floor. The brownstone is home to the Preston family, who became my surrogate family ten years ago. Conrad and Evelyn are in the penthouse on the top floor, and Raina, my best friend is on the second floor.

Entering the underground parking garage, William enters the code and parks in one of the guest parking spaces. Forgoing the elevator, William escorts me up the one flight of stairs to Wyatt's apartment.

Standing outside Wyatt's door, I ring the bell and wait. I'm ready to ring it again when the door swings open. Wyatt's eyes immediately move to the big hulking man behind me.

"William Mathers, Wyatt Preston. Wyatt Preston, William Mathers," I say quickly making the introductions. "William is my bodyguard."

William nods. "Mr. Preston," he says by way of greeting.

Mimicking William's nod, Wyatt steps aside, inviting me in.

"I'll only be about an hour or so," I tell William.

"Yes, Miss West. I'll wait for you in the garage. Please call me when you're ready to leave. I'll come and escort you down."

"I will. Thank you." He waits for me to step inside before walking away.

"So, you have a bodyguard now?" Wyatt questions, after locking the door.

"I do. Since the break-in at my apartment and the leak to the tabloids connecting my past to my present."

"Are you frightened by it? Is that why you have security with you everywhere you go?"

"No, I'll admit the break-in freaked me out a little. Knowing that someone was in my home touching my things was unnerving to say the least."

"Why the terminator if you're okay?"

"Lucian thinks having my own security detail makes sense."

Wyatt frowns at that. "What do you think?" he asks, not hiding his annoyance.

"I was reluctant at first. I didn't want anyone hovering over me or getting in my way while I'm trying to work. Now, I believe it's better to be safe than sorry."

"So, it's still freaking you out, all this crap with the press and the break-in?"

"No, not really. I don't feel threatened, and I can defend myself. It just feels good to know someone is looking out for me. That someone has my back."

"Is that why you moved in with Thorne?"

"No, it's not." Clearing my throat, I continue. "I moved in with him because I want to be with him. It has nothing to do with the bodyguard he provides. Although, being with him has made me feel safer than I ever have."

"What makes him better for you than I am?" I see the disappointment in his eyes, and I know it's time to set him straight.

"With him, I'm the best version of myself. We're better for each other. I can't explain the bond we share. The connection we feel for each other was instantaneous. We couldn't deny it and I don't want to. I love Lucian like I've never loved anyone before, and there will be no one after him. He's it for me."

"Well damn." Wyatt runs his hand through his hair. "I thought I at least had a shot at convincing you to try with me. To see if there's anything between us worth building on."

I take his hand in mine. "I love you as a brother, Wyatt. Like I love Raina as a sister. You're my family. What happened between us should never have happened. I never meant to give you mixed signals or false hope, and for that I'm truly sorry."

"I love you, you know, and not like a sister," he says, stroking his thumb across my knuckles. "I have for a long time. I hoped you'd grow to love me in the same way. Especially after the night we shared together. Now I know that's not going to happen." He releases my hand, meeting my gaze. "I can live with not getting the girl, if you're happy."

"I never thought I could be this happy, but I really am. Lucian makes me happy."

Wyatt nods his acceptance. "Okay," he says. "We can catch up on everything else over lunch."

I know this is his way of changing the subject. He no longer wants to hear about how happy I am with Lucian.

"This way." He points, and I follow him down the small hall of the foyer, to the living room.

"What are we having for lunch? I ask, following his lead. "I'm starved."

"Pizza," he smirks.

His gaze goes to the coffee table, and the pizza box. It's from the same place as the pizza he brought to my apartment all those months ago, when we slept together. I don't need to open the box to know it's the same pizza we shared that night.

A pang of guilt runs through me. Guilt over using someone I care about in a moment of weakness. Guilt over rubbing my happiness in his face, when clearly, for Wyatt this lunch is more than just two friends catching up.

"Maybe this isn't such a good idea. I should go."

"It's okay, Avery." Wyatt grabs my arm, as I turn to leave, causing me to flinch involuntarily. "I'm sorry," he says, releasing me. "I did all this before I understood your feelings for Thorne. Please don't go, we're family."

"Wyatt, I don't want to lead you on."

'You're not. I'm a big boy and you've made your feelings perfectly clear." He takes a seat on the couch. "There's something else you should know," he says, before opening the pizza box and taking a slice for himself.

I take a seat on the chair opposite him. "What is it that I should know?"

"I'm here for you. Whatever you need. If you need me to be a friend or a brother, I'll be that for you, but if you ever need more, I'll be that too."

I nod, accepting that only time will truly heal his broken heart. We move past the subject of love and relationships and onto safer topics.

Wyatt fills me in on his plan to attend Stanford Medical School in the fall and I tell him all about the movie deal in the works for my book. The conversation is easy, flowing effortlessly from one topic to the next, erasing some of the lingering tension.

We've been talking for nearly two hours when I notice the time.

"I need to get going. I have a deadline and more research to do."

Wyatt stands with me. "I'll walk you down. No need to call Hercules."

"Alright," I say, retrieving my purse from the table."

We take the stairs down to the garage. Wyatt stops before we reach the car when he sees William waiting for me.

Wyatt pulls me into his arms for a hug. "I'm going to say goodbye here," he says, before releasing me. "Don't be a stranger." His voice is pleading. "We should do this again soon."

"We will, but no pizza," I joke.

He holds up three fingers, a scout's promise. "I'll do my best to stay away from any topic remotely related to the night that shall not be mentioned." His smile is cocky when he kisses my cheek. "See you later, sis." With that he turns and walk away.

"You were never a boy scout!" I shout after him. His laughter echoes through the garage.

I walk the few feet it takes to reach the sedan. William opens the back-passenger door for me, and I climb in.

I notice his cell phone, when I hear him say, "Yes, sir, she's fine. We're leaving now." William's intense gaze rakes over me, no doubt validating his statement regarding my well-being, before ending the call. It only takes one guess to know he's speaking to Lucian.

"Where to Miss West?" William asks, once he's behind the wheel.

"Home."

"Yes, ma'am."

Moments after we pull into traffic my iPhone rings. Hearing our ringtone affects me in a way I never would have anticipated when Lucian and I chose the song. The lyrics to Jace Everett's Bad Things make me wet and needy for Lucian every time I hear it.

"Hello Lucky." My voice is a sultry whisper.

"Avery." He groans, and I know he's thinking of my wet center. "I needed to hear your voice."

"Are you having a bad day?"

"No, just a long day."

"Is that why you called, because you miss me?"

"That, and I want you wet for me when I get home."

I chuckle. The call is premeditated. He knows what the song does to me. "I always am."

"That you are." His voice is huskier, more sensual. "And, Rose Petal, don't touch yourself. Save it all for me." His command holds a promise of untold delights. "I'll see you soon, my rose petal."

"Yes, Sir," I say, ending the call.

I busy myself researching an article for the rest of the trip home. There are still a few hours to go before Lucian leaves the office. So, instead of letting my mind linger over something I can't have, I go back to work.

William parks the sedan, and opens the door for me, before I notice my surroundings. He escorts me to the penthouse, making sure it's secure before leaving.

I dive back into my work, welcoming the distraction from the throbbing need between my thighs. I'm so engrossed in my work that I don't hear when Lucian enters the penthouse.

My iPhone rings, singing the familiar tone. A quick look at the clock tells me it's half past six. My body shudders with anticipation. Lucian is near. I can feel him. I don't answer the phone. I let my body lead me to him. The closer I get to him, the stronger the pull, the lyrics of the song fueling my desire. I want to do bad things with you, Lucian. The song has become our mating call and I absolutely love it.

Chapter 2
Lucian

IT HAS BEEN THREE WEEKS since my parents told me about my biological father, Philip Hunter. By some cruel twist of fate, that same man is Avery's adoptive father. The son of a bitch who sold her to pay off a gambling debt and then abandoned her when she was fifteen. Telling Avery, who has become as essential to me as the air I breathe, was the hardest thing I will ever do. I know that I can never make up for what the bastards did to her. I can only try to make things better for her going forward. Starting with every news outlet reporting that bullshit about her. They have all recanted their lies and issued public apologies. One cable network refused and paid the price, it's no longer on the air. No one fucks with my woman and gets away with it.

I can feel her getting closer. My body hums with a desperate need to possess her, to hear her scream my name. She enters our bedroom, glowing from the light that radiates from deep within her. It's that beacon of light the draws me to her. I watch her slide her sundress off her shoulders and past her hips, letting it fall to the floor. Before I can take a step toward her, she runs to me, jumping into my arms. She wraps her legs around my hips. Nearly losing my balance, I recover quickly, holding her body close to me. Her mouth covers mine, devouring me, taking what she needs. I fucking love that she has become more demanding with her desires.

My cock throbs painfully hard inside my pants. She nips my lower lip, and my breath quickens. My body reacts to hers like a horny teenager with a girl for the first time. Cupping the back of her head, I deepen the kiss. I'm hungry for her, and I can't get enough.

Breathing heavily, she breaks the kiss, dropping her forehead to mine. I carry her to the bed, laying between her legs, I rest my cock against her panty-covered center. She lifts her hips, grinding against my shaft. Finding the friction she needs, her desire builds. Her body shudders against mine with her release.

"I waited as long as I could." Her lips press against my neck, thickens my cock even further. "But I still need your cock inside me. Fuck me, Lucian," she moans

"And I need to be inside you," I groan.

I pull myself away from her. Missing the softness of her body, I undress quickly. She licks her lips, locking her gaze on me with avid appreciation. I love that look in her eyes. The insatiable hunger there matches mine.

I join her in bed, urging her thighs apart. She welcomes me, spreading wide to accommodate me. I glide my fingers across her warm center, and her panties are soaked through. Tugging her panties to one side, I slide two fingers inside her slick wet heat. Her cunt tightens around my fingers, drawing them in deeper. "I love it when you're wet and ready for me," I growl. Craving a taste of her makes my mouth water. I plunge deeper, hitting her G-spot again and again, triggering another orgasm.

I bring my fingers to my mouth, tasting her sweet essence. "You're a delicacy, Rose Petal. You should be savored, but all I want to do is devour every inch of you." Leaning back on my haunches, I run my hands down the outside of her thighs. She lifts her hips, aiding me in slipping her panties off.

I crawl between her thighs, loving how she has spread her legs wide for me. Fisting my cock, I guide the throbbing head into her sweet wet cunt. Sliding in a few inches at a time, I let her adjust to me. Lifting her hands above her head, I restrain her with one hand.

Her wide-eyed gaze questions me. We have been strictly vanilla since the revelation about Philip. I didn't want to trigger a sleepwalking episode or nightmares. Three weeks have passed without any incidents, and I know we both crave bad things. I want to take my time and make love to her slow and gentle, but the need to take her hard and fast overwhelms me.

Thrusting forward, I bottom out, filling her completely.

"Tell me you want it the same way I do."

"I do," she whispers, and its music to my ears. The excitement and hope I feel hearing those two words is undeniable.

We fuck long and hard, until we're blind with pleasure. Like a mantra, she cries my name over and over. Her body trembles with her third orgasm and she falls apart. I fall over the edge with her, my body shuddering violently with my release. I spurt, once, twice, three times, filling her. Possessing her.

When I release her arms, she wraps them around my back, holding me tight. "I love you," she says softly, her lips brushing against my shoulder.

"I know, and I love you too, so much."

Pulling out of her, I roll onto my back. I hold Avery in my arms, craving the feel of her skin against mine. Her head rests on my chest, and I inhale her scent. A mixture of lavender and honey, and us. The combination is intoxicating.

"I had lunch with Wyatt today."

My body tenses at the mention of the jackass coveting what's mine.

"I know."

"We talked. I think he gets it now. How I feel about you, I mean," she says, her tone soothing and gentle. Her fingers glide across my stomach and the tension I feel evaporates.

"How do you feel about me?" I know, of course, but I love hearing her say it.

"Don't you know when a girl's in love?" she teases.

"Are you in love, Sweetness?

"Irrevocably. Undeniably."

With that my world is set right again. She is mine always and forever.

"Are you ready for dinner? Maggie was here, and she has prepared a meal for us."

"I can eat but let me get cleaned up first." Sitting up in bed, she moves away from me.

"I'm just going to mess you up again."

"Yes, but I like when you start with a clean slate. Five minutes is all I need."

Hopping out of bed, she pads to the bathroom. I hear the shower and I can't resist joining her. Five minutes becomes twenty-five.

We make our way down the hall to the kitchen. I grab a bottle of Pinot Grigio, while Avery takes our dinner out of the warmer. Sitting side by side at the breakfast bar we dine on chicken piccata, served over linguine with a mushroom sauce. It's one of my favorite dishes.

"This is delicious," Avery says, after taking a big mouthful.

"I'll tell Maggie you like it."

"If there's anything you want her to add to the grocery list, or anything you want her to prepare for dinner, just let her know. She usually does the shopping on Friday, for the following week."

"I'll keep that in mind, but your pantry has just about everything I can think of."

We chat over dinner, enjoying the comfort of being at home together. I tell her about my day, and she tells me about the new article she's researching. After dinner, we curl up on the couch. Avery tunes the television to a classic movie channel. I don't know if I have ever done this before. Just relaxing, being happy and content with the one I love. I know I loved Camille, but I'm learning there are many ways to love. What I feel for Avery is beyond anything I've ever felt for Camille. I lost a part of my heart to Avery, the first time I stared into those beautiful hazel eyes. The bond we share is deeper than anything I ever imagined. Finding her again ten years later only proves we are fated.

We're halfway through the movie when the fire alarm goes off in the building. Instinctively, I reach for Avery's hand, acting swiftly to ensure her safety. We hurry to the bedroom, retrieve our cell phones, and step into our shoes.

"It could be a false alarm, but we need to go." I take Avery's hand again, leading her to the front door.

Avery grabs the throw from the couch as we are leaving the penthouse. I shut the door, but I don't lock it. We hear the alarm broadcasting clearly in the stairwell. The fire emergency is occurring on the floor below the penthouse. The affected floor, the floor above, and below it must evacuate immediately. We take the stairs down to the lobby, exiting the building.

Once we're on the curb, Avery and I move across the street away from the building. A crowd of the building's tenants gather outside, waiting for the all-clear to go back to their homes. Avery drapes the throw over her shoulders, covering herself. My girl doesn't like the attention she gets from wearing only a pair of leggings and a tank top. She feels exposed. I pull her close to me, blanketing the throw over her shoulders and covering her hips. Within a few minutes, we hear the fire trucks approaching. Soon after, I see the flashing lights. We're outside nearly thirty minutes before we're given the all-clear by the fire department.

We wait in the lobby, while our neighbors crowd into the packed elevators. Once Avery and I step into the empty elevator, I enter the code for the penthouse.

"Hold the elevator," a distinctly male voice yells out.

Avery press the button to hold the door open. I pull her close, when a young man with a bubbly redhead following close behind him, joins us. He presses the button for the fifth floor. I glance at them briefly to see that he's staring at Avery. It takes every ounce of self-control to keep from knocking him the fuck out.

"You two new?" the fucker asks, his speech slurred.

I feel Avery tense in my arms. "No, I own the building." I didn't mean to pull that card but fuck it. He needs to know who he's dealing with.

That got the redhead's attention, who up until now seem content with twirling her hair around her finger. "The whole building?" she asks, her words equally slurred.

"Yes, the whole building," I say, my eyes never leaving the drunken asshole. "Including the fifth floor," I add, making Avery chuckle a little.

"It's all good man, we're just visiting a friend. Not trying to cause any trouble."

Tension fills the elevator for the next couple of floors, before the ass hat steps out, dragging the redhead behind him.

"Including the fifth floor." Avery's laughter cleanses the polluted air the couple left behind.

"That's right," I say, kissing the top of her head.

"I didn't know you own this building."

"My portfolio is diversified. It's not just publishing and telecommunication. I also own two vineyards. One in California and another in the south of France. The Pinot Grigio we had with dinner tonight was from the vineyard in France."

Avery gapes up at me, eyes wide. "Wow, Thorne. I know you're loaded. So, I'm not sure why you owning a vineyard shocks me, but it does."

"Two vineyards," I tease

The elevator opens into my foyer. I stop abruptly and Avery bumps into me.

"What's wrong?" Avery looks up at me with raised brows.

"Not sure," I say, taking a step towards the partially open door, leading into the penthouse. "I thought I closed the door behind us."

"It was probably one of the firemen, confirming that we had evacuated."

Her explanation makes sense. But I'm thinking the firemen probably didn't make it this far since the emergency was contained on the floor below us.

"Do you think someone is inside?" Avery grabs my arm, halting my steps.

"No. But wait here."

"If you think I'm just going to wait here, you're crazy."

"Avery," I sigh, kissing her forehead. "It may be nothing, but I need you to wait here while I go check it out."

"Lucian, if you go, I go." She takes my hand. "Together."

I open the door and we enter our home together. We check every room and all the closets. Nothing appears to be out of place, but I can't shake the feeling that someone has been here. I make a mental note to have Franklin and Mathers do a thorough search tomorrow. I lock up and set the alarm, before leading Avery to our bedroom.

"I'm going to make some calls before bed," I tell her, deciding not to wait until tomorrow to share my suspicions with Franklin.

"Do you want me to wait up for you?"

I give her my wickedest grin. "Do you mind if I wake you?"

"No, of course not." Her lips part expectantly, a soft moan escaping.

"Then, it doesn't matter." I kiss her deeply, conveying a promise of more to come.

I walk down the hall to my office, regretting that I've left Avery alone in bed. More than anything I want to give her the attention she craves. My focus is divided, and apprehension gnaws at me, robbing me of my concentration. Once I put my mind at ease, I can get back to what really matters. Avery.

I sit at my desk, turn on the lamp, and power on my iMac. The screen comes to life, displaying a photo of Avery and me. She had taken a selfie of the two of us while we were visiting the Montauk Lighthouse. She's as radiant as the sun setting in the background of the photo. I gaze at the screen with hungry eyes taking in the sight of her. The glow in her hazel green eyes mesmerizes me, and her luscious full lips are curled up in a smile. My body reacts, craving her kiss; a heart-stopping kiss that takes my breath away, while sustaining my life.

I send a quick email to Carter before calling Franklin. He will have to forgive me for disturbing him on his night off. I select the speed dial option. It rings twice before his gruff voice answers.

"The fire alarm went off in the building this evening. There was a small fire on the floor below the penthouse. I think it was deliberate."

"I'm on my way, sir." Franklin lives in my building; which is part of the perks of being my driver and bodyguard. I know he's not home tonight. His nights off are usually spent in Queens with the woman he's seeing.

"No need. There was no property damage and I've checked out the penthouse and nothing seem to be out of place. It just feels off."

"You believe someone was there, and used the fire to gain access?"

"My gut instinct tells me that's exactly what happened."

"It should be easy enough to prove. The security footage during the time you were out will show if someone entered the penthouse unauthorized. I'll contact Carter and have him send someone over to do a full sweep for listening devices and prints."

"I sent Carter an email. He'll be expecting your call first thing in the morning."

"Do you think this has anything to do with the break in at Miss West's apartment?"

"The thought had occurred to me. First a break in at Avery's, now here."

"It could be a coincidence."

"I don't believe in coincidences. Avery is the connection. Whatever is going on, she's at the center of it and I need answers."

"We'll get them, sir."

"Be here tomorrow morning at nine."

"Yes, sir," I hear him say before the line goes silent, ending the call.

Powering off the iMac and lamp, I leave the office. Padding quietly about the penthouse, I enter the bedroom, not wanting to disturb Avery, who is undoubtedly asleep by now. My gaze falls on the sleeping figure curled up on my side of the bed, hugging my pillow. I undress and join her in bed. I pull her into my arms, pillowing her head on my chest. She stirs in my arms and whispers, "Lucian."

My cock stiffens when she drapes her leg over my thigh, the warmth of her center heating my flesh.

"Go back to sleep," I say, contrary to my actions. I glide my hand down the small of her back and she whimpers.

"I'm not sleepy." Her voice is breathy and filled with need. Moving her hips, she grinds her clit against the muscles of my thigh. “I just want to feel you between my legs,” she confesses shamelessly. “Any part of you.”

“I can never deny you. I’ll always be the instrument of your pleasure.”

I roll onto my back, pulling her on top of me. She slides down my cock, my hands guiding her hips. I watch in awe, the way my cock disappears inside her warm wet cunt. Mesmerized as she covers me inch by inch, her cunt tightens around me. The vision is both erotic and beautiful.

She leans forward, her lips at my throat and she whisper, “You’re so hard, Lucky. And it feels so good, you stretching and filling me. You’re so deep.” She gasps.

My rose petal rides me fast and hard, building friction as she chase her release.

She’s so wet, and it feels unfuckingbelievable. Avery clenches around me, and I thrust deeper into her, trembling violently, my body seized with pleasure so intense, I forget to breathe. Our eyes lock, and the undeniable hunger I see in her eyes reflects mine.

“Lucian,” she cries. Her body shudders, triggering my own release and I fall over the edge with her, growling her name.

She collapses on my chest, breathing heavily. We lay like that until our breathing returns to normal. My now soft cock has slipped out of her, and she seems content with our current position. A few minutes later, the sound of her even breathing tells me she’s fast asleep. Rolling Avery onto her side, I hold her close, my front to her back. Turning off the bedside lamp, I fall asleep, cupping her breast.

Chapter 3
Avery

WHEN I AWAKE, LUCIAN is wrapped around me, cocooning me with his body. I try not to wake him, while freeing myself from his embrace. He stirs, rolling onto his back. His forearm rests above his head but his eyes are still closed. My gaze travels the length of his body, admiring his well-defined eight-pack and muscular arms. His erection outlines the white sheet draping his hips. He's the picture of perfection. I stare at him a moment longer, before leaving our bed.

I tiptoe to the bathroom, closing the door behind me. I use the toilet and brush my teeth, before stepping into the shower. A few minutes later, I'm showered and ready to tackle my hair. It's always a chore after it gets wet, the ends too curly to manage. I quickly blow dry my hair, then use my flat iron to straighten and style it. It takes me thirty minutes to tame my tangled tresses.

Lucian is still asleep when I return to our bedroom. The sheet has slipped from his hips, and he is sprawled out on his back in all his glory. His erection lay hard and thick against his abdomen. My breathing has become fast and audible, while his remains calm and steady. I desperately want to climb back into bed and have my way with him. To feel him deep inside me. I touch myself, imagining my hands are his. I close my eyes, and the memory of his lips and his touch warms my skin.

The towel wrapped around me falls to the floor. I cup my breast with my left hand, pinching my nipple. My right-hand slides down my stomach between my thighs. Spreading my legs, I stroke my swollen clit. I gasp when I sink two fingers into my soaking wet core. Slick wet fingers press hard on my throbbing clit. I feel my center clenching around my fingers desperately begging for release. I can't stop the tremors that wrack my body, even if I wanted to.

"Avery." Lucian's husky voice calls out to me.

I open my eyes and he's watching me. I'm so close and all I want is to shatter for him, to shatter with him.

"I want to watch you come. Get yourself off, Rose Petal." Lucian words cause a visceral reaction, and his heated gaze burns through me, melting my core.

"Imagine I'm touching you. Can you feel how much I want you? Can you feel your lover's hands on your body, worshipping you, caressing you, and making you wetter than you've ever been? Can you feel me?"

"Yes," I moan. My center tightens around my fingers, and my knees go weak. I cry out as my orgasm rips me apart. I feel myself falling, as strong arms wrap around me, holding me up. I shatter in Lucian's arms, whispering his name.

"You're so fucking beautiful when you come," he says, kissing my face, as my breathing slowly returns to normal.

"I was thinking of you. And I got so wet, but I didn't want to wake you."

"Whenever, wherever, and however. Remember."

I nod, remembering the terms we set at the beginning of our relationship.

"I'll always give you what you need." His lips brush against mine, sealing them in a toe-curling kiss.

"All I need is you," I say, breaking the kiss. "And what do you need now?" I ask, looking down at his rock-hard cock pressing against my belly.

"I have forty-five minutes before Franklin and Mathers arrive."

"That's plenty of time."

"Oh, really. For what?

"For us to hop in the shower and start the morning together."

I squeal when Lucian scoops me up into his arms and carries me into the bathroom. He sits me on the edge of the tub, while he uses the toilet. I've become accustomed to him being so uninhibited when it comes to how he shares his body with me.

I turn on the shower head and adjust the temperature so it's just right. I step into the shower for the second time this morning. Lucian joins me after brushing his teeth. Standing behind me, he pulls me into his arms.

"Place your hands against the wall," he commands. "I'll try not to wet your hair," he whispers, kissing me tenderly on my neck when I comply.

"I'd appreciate that," I say, knowing it's a promise he won't keep."

I lean into him, his cock pressing hard into my back. His hand glides over my hip, slipping between my thighs and spreading my legs. Skilled fingers part my folds, sinking deep inside my center. I moan; it feels so good being surrounded by him.

"Fuck my fingers, Sweetness. Make yourself come." My center tightens around his fingers at the gentle command.

My hips move frantically, grinding against his hand. Lucian cups my breast, squeezing it, then he pinches my nipple between his fingers. I cry out. The tinge of pain is tempered by the pleasure of his tongue circling my ear. His deep seductive voice pushes me closer to the edge.

"There's nothing better than being inside you. It's my favorite place."

Tremors of excitement course through my body, fueling my desire, making me wetter. His words have that power over me. The power to penetrate deep into the heart of me, triggering my release.

"Turn around, Rose Petal." I do as he commands.

Facing him, I see the need in his eyes; the raging hunger that promises to consume me. I watch him lift his come slick fingers to his lips, drawing them into his mouth. His eyes never leaves mine. "You are everything I crave. I'll never have my fill of you."

I smile, and feminine pride makes me step closer. "I feel the same way about you, Lucian."

He cups my ass, lifting me off my feet. "Wrap your legs around me." Once again, I obey, clinging to him. My back is pressed to the cold tile of the shower wall. Lucian lowers his head, covering my mouth with his.

We're both panting when Lucian breaks the kiss. Red hot passion heats my blood. The desire to submit to his will intoxicates me. I gasp when his cock slips into me, stretching me and filling me one delicious inch at a time. "My god, woman, you feel so fucking good." His voice is a low growl.

Lucian's moves are calculated, moving slow and deep, drawing out my pleasure. I press my lips to his neck, licking and kissing him. My teeth graze his chin, urging him to pick up the pace. Thrusting upward, Lucian pulls me down against him and fills me wholly. We move together, both completely consumed by the other. Our grunts and moans mingling create an exquisite symphony.

His possession pushes me over the edge, and I explode around him. He follows me, and his release triggers small tremors in me. We sink to the floor, holding each other tightly. Straddling him, I tilt my chin up and he seizes my mouth in a kiss.

"We should take an actual shower," I say, resting my head on his chest. "I'm a prune and my hair is a poufy mess."

"If you insist," he says, twirling my hair. "I like the way your hair feels on my fingers. I like how it feels in my hands when I make love to you."

His candid confessions always takes me by surprise, revealing more of himself to me every day. "I love all the ways you love me. How you love me so intensely." I sigh and let the truth of my words move me forward. "I love how loving you has made me stronger and more confident."

"I love you, Avery."

"I love you too, Lucian. Always."

"Always," he repeats

We stand, cleansing each other before turning off the water. I follow Lucian out of the shower. He wraps me in a towel and pats me dry, before doing the same for himself.

Fifteen minutes later, we're at the breakfast bar enjoying egg white omelet, fresh fruit, and coffee. Since I moved in, Maggie is only here four days a week. Lucian and I fend for ourselves on the weekends and Wednesdays. With guests coming for dinner tonight, I'm glad I'll have her help in the kitchen.

"Are you working from home today?"

"I thought I might," Lucian responds. "There are a few things here that require my attention."

"Are you still concerned that someone may have entered the penthouse last night?"

"I am." He pauses. "I don't believe in coincidences. Your apartment a few weeks ago, now this. I can't shake the feeling that something is off."

"You think the two are related?"

"I'm not sure, but I want to rule out every possibility, which is why Franklin and Mathers will be here shortly."

"I see."

"My first priority is to ensure your safety. I won't let anything happen to you."

"You know I can defend myself, right?"

"I'm aware of your self-defense training."

"Yes, there's that. But I also know how to use a gun and a knife."

Lucian looks at me, stunned silent. "That I didn't know."

"After I moved in with the Prestons, I became obsessed with self-defense. Firearms, close combat, hand-to-hand, and knife fight combat. It was difficult at first. I couldn't stand for anyone to crowd me or even touch me. But I stuck with it, and the more I learned the more I liked it. It gave me the self-confidence I needed to be a part of the world again."

"My girlfriend's badass."

I laugh. "Hardly! It still took me years to let my guard down and allow someone to get close to me."

"You didn't date after college?"

"I dated, but there was never anyone I wanted to date twice." My throat tightens with emotions. "I think I was always waiting for you to come back for me," I whisper.

"I want you so fucking much right now," he groans. "It makes me so happy that we found each other. From the moment I saw you in Vegas I was drawn to you. The craving and the need to possess you was so overwhelming. When you left my room, I woke looking for you and wanting you. I still hadn't realized what was happening to me. You had given me life. I felt alive for the first time in three years. And more alive than I've ever been in my life. I had to find you, and nothing was going to stop me."

"When I found out it was you who had taken me to the hospital that night, that it's your T-shirt I wear when I feel alone, it all made sense. I felt safe in your arms all those years ago. And when you held me in Vegas, my body reacted instinctively to the memory of being held in your arms. When I realized I was falling in love with you, I had to admit to myself that I've loved you ever since I walked out of that hospital with a single yellow rose, wearing your T-shirt.

"That night I just wanted you to be safe. I wanted to protect you. But my hands were tied, and the doctors wouldn't tell me anything. Now, I still want to protect and keep you safe. I also want to possess every inch of you, claim you, and make you mine.

"I'm yours, Lucian."

"And I'm yours." Leaning in, he gives me a chaste kiss.

The sound of the vacuum cleaner bursts our intimate bubble. Maggie is cleaning the penthouse and soon Franklin and William will be here working with Lucian.

I clear the dishes after breakfast and load the dishwasher, before Lucian and I retreat to separate home offices.

Nearly an hour into researching my article, Lucian appears in the doorway. "Come with me. I want you to see something."

"Sure, give me a moment to bookmark this page." I look up from my MacBook and see the urgent nature of his request. "Is everything okay?" I ask, stepping from behind the desk to Lucian's side."

"We have the surveillance footage from outside the penthouse last night." I follow him to his office, where Franklin and Mathers are waiting.

The two men stand when I enter the room. "Miss West," they say, almost in unison.

"Good morning Franklin, William." I greet them before sitting in one of the two chairs in front of Lucian's desk.

The iMac screen is facing me, and Lucian plays the recording for me. It starts with a view of the penthouse's foyer. Then a fireman appears and enters the penthouse. The time lapse says he was inside for about ten minutes. The video then shows a group of firemen on the floor below us. They seem to be checking the apartments. They are only inside each unit no more than a couple of minutes, maybe less. I also notice the uniform is different. The video ends and I sit in silence trying to process what this all means. Lucian takes a seat in the chair next to me, reaching for my hands.

"Avery are you okay?" he asks.

"I'm not sure. I was hoping there was nothing to this."

"I know."

"What now?"

"Franklin and Mathers are on it." I look around the room and see they have left us alone. "They've already checked the penthouse for listening devices and hidden cameras." I gasp. The thought of someone listening in or watching Lucian and me makes me feel ill. "The place is clean. The alarm codes have been changed, and there will be 24—hour security stationed in the foyer until further notice. Three men from Thorne Security will be here soon and they will work in eight-hour shifts. I want you to meet them, to be aware of their presence outside our home."

I want to respond, to say something, but the words are trapped in my throat. I know that the break-in at my Chelsea apartment and this violation of privacy are related. I also know that I'm what both incidents have in common. Both are places I call home. I won't just sit back and be victimized again. I'm no longer that frightened fifteen-year-old girl.

"Should we cancel our dinner plans for tonight?" I ask, concerned I might be putting our family and friends in danger.

His understanding gaze meets mine. "Only if you want to. There's no evidence to say that anyone is in any physical danger."

I consider his words before responding. "I want to have our friends over for dinner, but I don't want to be the reason anyone gets hurt."

"Sweetness." Lucian pulls me into his arms, and I relax against his chest, absorbing his strength. "If it makes you feel better, I'll assign security to our families until this is resolved."

I stare at him in awe, this amazing man, my man. "You will do that for me?"

"You should know by now that I'll do anything for you."

"Yes." I nod because I know in my heart that he speaks the truth. He'll do anything for me, just as I'll do anything for him. "Will you keep me in the loop? I don't want to be kept in the dark about any of this."

"As soon as there's any new information, you'll be the first to know."

"Thank you."

"And dinner?" Lucian asks. "Are we hosting our first dinner party tonight?"

"We are." I try to hide the anxiety I feel about getting to know his sister and friends better. "I'm looking forward to it."

"They're going to love you." As always, Lucian sees through me. "You already have so much in common with Katelyn and Marcus. They're both artists, but did you know that Marcus is also a writer and Katelyn plays the piano?"

I smile, loving his attempt to make me feel at ease. "What about Jake? Do we have anything in common?"

"Yes, you both love Raina," Lucian says.

"And we both love you," I add.

"There's also that," he smiles.

"I would go as far as to say that loving you is what we all have in common."

I lean into him because I can't help myself. I kiss him tenderly, savoring the feel of his lips on mine. The kiss is undemanding at first. Lucian pulls me onto his lap, and I straddle him. Placing his hand at the back of my head, he holds me in place, deepening the kiss. His cock grows harder against my center. Rocking back and forth, I find my rhythm. He captures my moans, swallowing my cries of pleasure. I want to pull my damp panties to the side and fill my aching center with his thick hard cock. Lucian thrusts up, holding my hips down, grinding into me. The friction is enough to send me over the edge. I writhe against him, chasing my release.

"Oh god!" I cry.

"That's it, come for me," he growls. "Come for me now."

Shattering into a million pieces, I fall apart in his arms. My breathing returns to normal and I rest against his chest, sated and happy.

"Feel better?" he asks, kissing my forehead.

"What about you? You didn't come."

"I'll be fine," he says, his voice normal again. "This was for you."

"Thank you."

"No need to thank me, Sweetness. Your needs are mine to fulfill."

I lift my chin, offering my mouth to him. Lucian's mouth descends on mine, kissing me with renewed passion.

Chapter 4
Lucian

AVERY AND I STAY IN my office for another half hour, making out like a couple of horny teenagers. She kisses me, touching and arousing me beyond belief. As much as I want to bend her over my desk and have my wicked way with her, I hold myself in check, letting her take the lead.

A tap at the door interrupts us, reminding me that we have business to attend to. I pull my mouth away from hers. She moans and nips my bottom lip, expressing her disappointment.

"The security team is here. We need to meet with them."

"Five more minutes," she pleas. Her breath warms my skin and tickles my neck. When her hands glide up to my hair and her lips brush across mine all thoughts of work vanishes.

Fifteen minutes later and we're adjusting our clothes. "To be continued, Miss West," I say, leading Avery out of my office to the living room.

Avery and I join Franklin and Mathers, along with three new members of the security team. I make quick introductions, before getting down to business, going over the parameters of their assignment. Franklin takes them on a tour of the building, including the service elevator and the garage. Mathers continues viewing the security footage, leaving Avery and I to tend to other matters. She returns to her research, and I go back to my office. Avery and I agreed that the extra security measures will begin at 6 a.m. tomorrow morning. We don't want to alarm our guests unnecessarily tonight.

• • • •

A FEW HOURS LATER, Katelyn is the first of the dinner guests to arrive. She greets me with a hug. My sister has dark hair like me, but where my eyes are blue, hers are a deep chocolate brown like our mother's. She's three years younger than me, and when she was born, she connected our family in a way the adoptions never did. She's the anchor that grounds the Thorne family.

"I brought wine," she says, shoving the bottle into my hand. "Where's Avery?"

"She'll be out soon," I say, leading her into the living room. "Would you like a drink?"

"Whatever you're having."

"Scotch."

"Neat?" she asks

"Is there any other way to drink Macallan or any decent single malt scotch?"

"You sound like dad." She laughs, taking the offered drink.

"A true gentleman and a connoisseur of fine scotch." I hold up the bottle of Macallan 30, showing it to her. "Dad gave me a bottle on my thirtieth birthday. It's long gone, but I keep it stocked."

"The man gives awesome gifts."

"That he does," I say. "He's taking mom to Italy for their anniversary."

"I know, she couldn't stop squealing about it when she found the itinerary."

"Shit! He wanted to surprise her."

"When has anyone ever been able to surprise mom?"

"You have a...."

Avery enters the room, and the sight of her stops my heart. Her gaze is focus on me. Crossing the width of the room, she walks into my arms. She tilts her chin, offering me her mouth. A gesture that's come to mean an offer of submission. We didn't have time to finish what she started in my office earlier today. The look in her eye tells me she's craving my attention. I cover her mouth, and she moans into mine. I fucking love that sound. I break the kiss. There's no need to give my little sister a show.

"Katelyn's here," I say, stroking her cheek tenderly.

Avery turns in my arms, facing Katelyn. "I'm so sorry. I didn't see you there," Avery says, apologizing.

"Don't ever apologize for making my brother happy." Katelyn grabs Avery in a tight hug. Yes, my sister is a hugger. "Seeing Lucian happy is the best thing ever."

"Without the PDA," Avery adds, and they both giggle."

"Would you like a drink, Sweetness?"

"A glass of wine, please. But I need to plate the hors d'oeuvres first," she says, before leaving to join Maggie in the kitchen.

"She's great, Lucian," Katelyn says, once Avery is far enough away that we aren't overheard. "And I can tell she really loves you."

"I really love her," I admit. "I can't imagine ever being without her."

"Don't do that."

"Do what?"

"Make yourself crazy with the what ifs."

It has always been easy to talk to my sister. She's wise beyond her years. She knows that my fear of losing Avery is born out of betrayal. Fear that Avery will betray me like Camille did, like our brother Daniel did.

I nod in acquiescence and change the subject. "How's the art gallery opening coming along?"

"Amazing," she beams. "The studio above the gallery is perfect. And I already have a few local artists all set to exhibit their work on opening night."

"What about your own work? Will any of it be showcased?"

"I have a few pieces that will be included. So does Marcus."

"He told me he was painting again. Is that your influence?"

Katelyn could get Marcus to do almost anything. I remember when she was fifteen, she wanted to go to some art show at MoMa and the only person she could talk into taking the train with her was Marcus. Growing up we were all very close. My friends became her friends and then they became family. Katelyn and Marcus seemed to drift apart after his parents died. He didn't spend as much time around the house and then he went away to college. While Marcus and I have remained as close as brothers, he and Katelyn only see each other on occasion.

"I don't have any influence over Marcus," she snaps. "He does as he pleases."

Before I can question her statement, Raina, Jake, and Marcus walk in. I make a mental note to find out if there's an issue between Katelyn and Marcus.

Katelyn excuses herself, strides over to the bar, and pours herself another drink.

I join Avery at the entrance, greeting the rest of our guests. We all gather in the living area. Maggie has set out the hors d'oeuvres, and Jake is playing bartender. Avery, Raina, and Katelyn are standing near the breakfast bar, chatting like they are all old friends. As usual Marcus is trying hard not to notice my sister. He's had it bad for her since we were teenagers. He tries to hide it, but we all know. I respect that he didn't try to date her back then. My best friend dating my kid sister would have fucked up our friendship. We were all he had. Now that we're all adults, I can't think of two people more suited for each other. Except Avery and I of course.

The dinner party is underway, and Avery is the perfect hostess, socializing with everyone. My gaze follows her around the room, willing her to turn and see me. To see the suppressed desire in my eyes. Being near her sparks a fire in me. The way her hips sway when she moves, the laughter that cause her breasts to rise and fall, and the sexy-as-fuck smile she gives me when she catches me staring.

"Fuck," I murmur to myself, hoping no one heard me over the conversations taking place.

"What's up?" Jake asks, amused by my heated tone.

"Just wishing it was three hours later."

"So, you haven't figured out how to control time?" he teases at my expense. "What can I do to help speed it up?"

"Leave," I say, and he breaks into a full-on laugh.

"Raina would kill me. Seeing Avery and this dinner party is all she's talked about all week."

"Well, I suppose I can endure your presence a little longer. I wouldn't want Avery's best friend to go to prison for murdering my best friend, would I?"

"I do appreciate your sacrifice."

"What are friends for?"

"Saving my life apparently." His gaze follows mine to Avery. "How have you two been? Have there been any other problems since you got back from the beach house?"

"There was an incident last night." I feel the tension coming off him immediately. "It's being handled, everything is under control."

"What happened?"

I share all the details with him. From the fire alarm, my suspicion that someone entered the penthouse, the security footage confirming it, and the additional safety measures I have implemented. Jake listens silently, while I tell him that I believe someone is targeting Avery.

"Do you have any suspects? Any leads at all?"

"Not a goddamn one," I say, my harsh words revealing my frustration.

"I could use another drink. How about you?" Jake offers.

Marcus joins us, and Jake pours another round of scotch for the three of us. A loud crash coming from the kitchen followed by Katelyn and Raina's yelling out for help has the three of us moving lightning fast.

"She needs her EpiPen." Raina's terrified gaze meets mine.

I'm on the move again, racing down the hall to our bedroom. I find Avery's purse there, on the bed, but no EpiPen. I hurry to the bathroom, searching the medicine cabinet, again no EpiPen and no Benadryl. I grab her purse, my keys and wallet, and race back to the kitchen.

I kneel on the kitchen floor, taking Avery from Raina's arms. "Both EpiPens are missing. I need to get her to the hospital."

"I'm coming with you."

I nod, passing Avery's purse to her. I hold Avery close, carrying her out of the penthouse.

"Katelyn, call Franklin and tell him to meet us at the hospital." She pulls out her phone before the elevator closes, taking us to the roof.

I don't have time to appreciate the shocked expression on Raina's face when she realizes I'll be piloting the helicopter. Avery's airways have become constricted and she's having difficulty breathing. Her eyes and lips are swollen and she's in and out of consciousness. I strap them both in securely and slam the door shut. I take my seat and buckle up. I grab two headsets and pass them to Raina.

"Put these on," I say before covering my ears.

I do a preflight check, and everything looks good. The tower gives me clearance and I'm ready. Pulling back on the throttle, we rise effortlessly.

Avery vomits twice during the flight, and I thank the universe for Raina and the care she's giving her.

The hospital's helipad is visible, and I prepare to land. While powering down, I notice hospital personnel approach as the blades come to a stop.

"Mr. Thorne," the female doctor yells over the noise.

I unbuckle the harness, open the door, and climb out of the seat onto the helipad. "I'm Lucian Thorne, and this is Avery West."

"Your sister called ahead. I have an EpiPen, and we can take her down to the ER for further treatment." She has two younger doctors at her side with a gurney.

Raina climbs out, joining the four of us on the helipad. The doctor climbs in, injecting Avery with the EpiPen. After Avery is strapped to the gurney, we are led to the elevator.

Raina and I keep pace with the doctors, running through the hospital to the ER.

The female doctor stops us. "This is as far as you go. Please wait here while we treat her."

"I'm not leaving her side!" I bark.

"Mr. Thorne, you reacted quickly getting Miss West here so fast. Now, let me do my part. I can assure you she's in capable hands."

I listen calmly, undeterred by her words. Nothing and no one will keep me from being at Avery's side. I'm reminded of the night ten years earlier, when the doctor wouldn't tell me anything or let me see her. That will not happen today.

"By all means doctor, do your part, treat her. Because if she doesn't get better, and you are responsible, by delaying her treatment. I will buy this fucking hospital and make sure you never practice medicine again."

"Mr. Thorne, I understand that you're upset and worried for Miss West. But I'm afraid my hands are tied in this matter. It's hospital policy."

Raina steps forward. "Miss West is my sister and Mr. Thorne is her boyfriend. If you need family consent, I give it."

The doctor gives us both a skeptical look, and just then Franklin arrives, followed by Jake.

"You can lead the way or get out of my way." I look past the doctor to Jake. "Either way you should meet my attorney, Jacob Gannon."

With that I hurry past the doctor, to where Avery is being treated.

The first thing I see is a machine hooked up to her, helping her breathe. Fear and anger wrestle inside me. Fear that I could lose her, and anger at the son of a bitch responsible for her being here. Deep down I know the latter is true. This is no fucking coincidence. Both EpiPens went missing on the same fucking day she somehow comes in contact with the one thing she's allergic to. A goddamn nut. No fucking way that's coincidental.

"She's sedated." The doctor appears behind me. "She had a severe reaction. She just needs rest now. The swelling has started to go down and as soon as she's breathing on her own, we can remove all this." She gestures toward the machines and I.V. tube in her hand.

"I want her moved to a private room. My security team will be here shortly to ensure her safety."

"I'll make the necessary arrangements," she says, before leaving me alone with Avery.

Outside the private recovery room, I meet with Franklin and Mathers.

"This was a deliberate act to hurt Avery. Whoever entered the penthouse somehow knows about her nut allergy. I want every item of food checked for contamination. Start with the food that was prepared for tonight's dinner. Maggie is aware of Avery's allergy but talk to her. Cover all the bases. I need to know who's doing this and why."

Avery has been breathing on her own for about two hours now. While I don't intend to leave, everyone else seems content to wait with me. She stirs, opening her eyes slowly, squinting against the glare of the lights.

"Lucian." Her voice is a raspy whisper, but it sounds like heaven.

"I'm here, Sweetness."

"You have a helicopter." It's not a question. "And you can fly a helicopter."

I chuckle. "How are you feeling? I ask, lowering my head to kiss her.

Her gaze travels over all the worried faces in the room. "Hungry."

"The doctor said you need to drink plenty of fluids to replenish your electrolytes. And you need to take it easy for a few days."

Avery tries to sit up in bed, but she winces in pain. "Ouch, that hurts."

"The doctor said you will experience some pain for a few days, and you may have some difficulty walking."

"I remember the side effects of using an EpiPen."

"Okay, for the next week you need to rest, and avoid any type of activity that could cause you to become exhausted, as it could trigger another attack."

Her eyes roam over my body. "All activities," she whispers, so that only I hear it.

I smirk. "Rest and well-balanced healthy meals while you're recovering. No physical activities."

"Yes, Sir," she whispers again, knowing how those words affect me when she speaks them.

"Behave," I command gently. "Franklin will be here soon with some soup. In the meantime, you have people waiting to see you."

She nods and pouts, looking so sexy it almost makes me forget my vow to handle her gently for the next few days.

I step aside, allowing Raina and Katelyn to sit and visit with her.

"How is she?" Marcus asks.

"She's sore and hungry, but otherwise fine."

"How long does she have to stay in the hospital?"

"I can take her home tomorrow, as long as there are no complications overnight."

Marcus, Jake, and I stand there, taking in the sight of our women, laughing and smiling. Avery's gaze meets mine and I know I'm looking into the eyes of the woman I'm going to spend the rest of my life with.

Chapter 5
Avery

I AM EXHAUSTED BY THE time Raina and Jake leaves. Katelyn and Marcus were the first to go. Now that I've eaten and assured everyone, I'm okay, I can scarcely keep my eyes open. Lucian hasn't left my side, and his worried expression tells me he doesn't intend to.

"Are you staying with me tonight?" I ask, barely containing my yawn.

"I am."

"Where are you going to sleep?"

His brow lifts and I want to take back the foolish question. "Are you kicking me out of your bed, Avery?"

"No, but aren't you worried I might over-exert myself?"

"Why would sleeping make you tired?"

"Because I'm going to do everything I can to finish what we started in your office."

"You're planning to test my resolve; you want to try to break me. Is that it, Miss West?"

"That's the plan."

"Care to place a wager on it?"

All kinds of warning bells go off, but I ignore them. "What do you have in mind?"

"Just a friendly bet. If you can get me to fuck you tonight, you can choose your prize. And when I win, I will choose mine."

"If you win, can I refuse to pay if I don't like the prize you choose?"

"You have your safe word, use it if you need to. I won't stop you."

I'm not sure I want to take this bet. My safe word has come to mean more than just a way to put a stop to the bad things I let him do to me. It's come to represent who he is to me. My lighthouse, my safe place. Keeping me safe has always been his priority. My safe word now serves dual purposes and that's okay.

"I accept your terms, Mr. Thorne."

"Then we have a deal, Miss West."

Lucian removes his shoes and socks before climbing into the small hospital bed with me. He lies on his side, my head pillowing his shoulder. I breathe him in, and his scent is more potent than any drug. The minty breeze of his toothpaste and the warm woodsy fragrance of sandalwood from his body wash. I press my nose to his neck and take a deep breath. Reaching up, I stroke his cheek.

"Will you kiss me goodnight?" I ask, lifting my chin.

Lucian gives me a chaste kiss on my lips and pulls away. "Good night, Avery."

"You're really not going to make love to me?"

"No, your body can't handle the exertion right now." His voice trembles with passion he's fighting to control. "You have no idea how much I want you, and all the things I want to do to you. But you can't handle it and I won't jeopardize your health."

"Tell me," I murmur. My panties are wet just imagining all the possibilities. "Tell me all the things you want to do to me," I whisper in his ear.

"Oh, Sweetness," he groans, his voice deep with desperate longing.

I press my lips to his, and he hesitates for a moment, before reciprocating. My tongue meets his, hardening his cock against my stomach.

Lucian's lips tremble against mine, barely containing his growing desire. "No," he whispers. "You need to rest."

"I need you." I hear the desperation in my voice. My fingers glide over the outline of his bulging cock, scarcely restrained in his pants.

Lucian groans, pressing his cock against my hand. "I need you, Lucian. Please."

"I need you too." His mouth captures mine. It's a hungry, needful kiss. Our teeth clash, desperate to satisfy our mutual craving.

Lucian's hand skims down my body, resting it between my thighs. My pulse race with anticipation. His fingers circle my clit through the damp cotton panel of my panties. I moan when the ache between my thighs builds.

I shift in Lucian's arms, grinding slightly against his palm. His fingers glide over my center to the edge of my panties, stroking my inner thigh. I try to keep my breathing under control. I don't want to give Lucian any reason to stop.

"Lucian," I whisper, begging for all the things his touch promises.

His lips caress my ear, his lustful voice, exuding carnal desire, makes me shudder. "I want to fuck you. I want to be buried deep in your sweet cunt all night. I want to tease you and make you beg for my cock. I want to hear you scream my name. I want to make you come harder than you ever have. Do you know why Avery?" he asks, sliding his fingers under the edge of my panties.

My breathing has become erratic, his words blazing a fiery trail of passion, heating my core. I don't answer his question, but we both know it's because I'm his.

"You're so wet for me," he groans. "Tell me you'll take what I give you," he demands.

"Yes. Please, yes." My center tightens around the two fingers Lucian slides in my sopping wet pussy. He massages my G-spot, over and over, finger fucking me, pushing me closer to the edge.

Lucian's teeth graze my chin before biting my lower lip. The flash of pain sparks my release. I come fiercely, shattering in his arms, my body seizing around his fingers, drawing him in deeper. I cry out his name, euphoric and sated. Lucian covers my face with tender kisses and my breathing slowly returns to normal.

"I love you, Avery." Lucian's breathing is slightly uneven. "I'd do anything to keep you safe. That includes making sure you follow doctor's orders. I want to make love to you, and I will when you're feeling better. Until then, I want you to rest. You could have died today. And the thought of life without you is..."

I place a finger over his lips, silencing him. "I love you so much, it hurts. I can't imagine my life without you either. I want you so much sometimes, the craving overwhelms me, and I can't think straight. And I just want to feel you inside me. I want to feel you losing control. I need to know that you crave us as much as I do. That you..."

"Christ, Avery, don't you know how I feel about you? Saying I love you doesn't begin to cover the depths of my feelings. I'd fucking die for you, even kill for you. You're my addiction; a craving that consumes me with a hunger that only you can satisfy. I'm fucking obsessed with you. I'll never let you go."

"So, you're saying you really really love me?" I tease.

"I'm saying you're the blood in my veins, the air that I breathe, and you're mine, always."

Safe in Lucian's arms, the dim light and the hum of the machines lulls me to sleep.

• • • •

LUCIAN IS NOWHERE TO be found when I awake alone. With an urgent need to pee, I climb out of bed and pad barefoot to the bathroom. I flip the light switch on the wall, illuminating the sterile environment. After relieving myself, I wash my hands and head back to the room.

When Lucian arrives ten minutes later, I'm sitting up in bed.

"I was hoping to get back before you woke," he says, kissing me on my forehead. "Good morning, beautiful. I wanted to surprise you with breakfast."

My stomach growls and I realize how hungry I am. The last time I had a meal was yesterday at lunchtime. "Good morning," I echo his greeting. "I'm starved. What did you bring me?"

"All your favorites." He smiles. "Special delivery from the chef at Thorne Tower. I figure my cafeteria food is much better than the hospital's cafeteria food."

Lucian pulls the tray table up to the bed. Unpacking the food, he places coffee, orange juice, eggs, bacon, croissants, and fresh fruit for two on the tray. I bite into the buttery goodness of the croissant and moan.

"It's delicious," I moan again after a second bite.

Lucian stares at me, his gaze as ravenous as my appetite. It's a look I recognize – his need to devour and possess me.

I tear off a piece of my croissant, offering it to him. "Would you like a taste?" I lick my bottom lip, enticing him further. I can't stop the rush of feminine pride that swells within me, his reaction triggers.

Lucian grasps my wrist, lowering his head, his mouth covering my fingers. I whimper when his tongue glides over my skin. His heated gaze holds me in a trance and I'm unable to look away even if I wanted to. He slips his tongue between my finger, freeing the small piece of croissant. He chews and swallows the tiny morsel. "I've tasted better," he says, licking his bottom lip, repeating my earlier gesture.

Those three words flow straight to my center, clenching my muscles, reminding me that I need to change my damn panties. I press my thighs together, attempting to satisfy the pressure building there.

Lucian's knowing smile only draws attention to his gorgeous mouth, and the fact he's enjoying my torment. My mind clings to the thought of his mouth on me, tasting me. For a moment, I'm blind to my surroundings. My back instinctively arches, when I recall the feel of Lucian's mouth wrapped around my nipples, licking and sucking them. The balance of pleasure and pain sent me spiraling over the edge. I groan, the memory is so vivid. The sound of Lucian's voice brings me back to the here and now.

"Are you okay, Sweetness?" His smirk says he's won this round.

"I...I'm okay. I was just wondering when I can go home." It's half true.

"Your doctor will come to give you a final exam soon and then we can go home. In the meantime, try to relax and eat your breakfast."

I follow Lucian's advice and try to relax. Unfortunately, the subject we've been avoiding keeps needling me. And I don't know how long we can put off talking about it. We need to deal with the fact that someone is trying to hurt me.

"I believe whoever entered the penthouse on Thursday is after me. Whoever it was took my EpiPens. That's a clear indication that this person means to harm me." I clear my throat and meet Lucian's gaze. "Or worse."

"I won't let anyone hurt you ever again," he vows.

"You can't protect me from the unknown. We don't even know who we're dealing with or the motivation behind any of this."

"I'll keep you safe or die trying."

I see the magnitude of his love and hear the strength of his words. He loves me enough to sacrifice everything, including his own life.

"Maybe I should move out for a little while. I don't want anyone else in harm's way."

"That's not going to happen," he says adamantly.

"It would kill me if anything happened to you"

"And I would die without you. Don't you know that?"

"I don't want to be any further away from you than I am now. I love you, Lucian Thorne, but you need to be reasonable."

"Love isn't reasonable."

"I'm afraid that whoever this person is will hurt you." I hold back the tears that threaten to fall. "Or worse. I'm not your obligation, you don't owe me anything."

"You are mine, Avery, and I am yours. That makes you my obligation, my obsession, and my world. Lucian reaches out and wipes away the single tear that has fallen to my cheek. "What we have is a fucking force of nature, it can't be stopped or contained. We'll get through this together. Do you understand, we're in this together?"

"I do." My voice cracks, and the tears I've been holding back break free.

Lucian pulls me into his arms, and I sob freely, letting go the anxiety that I've carried around since the break-in at my Chelsea apartment. Whatever comes Lucian and I will deal with it together.

Soon after, the doctor comes in to examine me and I'm given the okay to go home. We ride home in silence. I don't mind, we've said all we needed to about our current state. Lucian has added two additional cars for security. One car leads, and the other follows, each car containing two armed men. I've learned that the men who work for Thorne Security are ex-military, special forces or Navy Seals. With all this security, I feel like a visiting foreign dignitary. It's a little claustrophobic to say the least. The limo comes to a stop, and we wait while our armed guards secure the area.

"All clear," Franklin says, opening the door for Lucian.

Lucian climbs out, offering me his hand. We walk to the elevator flanked by Franklin, Mathers, and the three new guys, whose names I have not yet committed to memory.

Maggie is waiting for us in the foyer when the elevator opens. Which is odd, since she doesn't work on the weekend.

She approaches us sobbing. "I'm so sorry, Miss West," she apologizes through a flood of tears.

I wrap my arms around her, comforting her. "It's okay. This wasn't your fault." I lead her into the living area. I sit with her on the couch until her tears have stopped.

"You shouldn't be taking care of me," she sniffles. "How are you feeling? Do you want to lie down and rest for a while?"

"I'm fine. Nothing a soak in the tub and a few hours of sleep in my own bed won't fix."

"We've restocked the pantry and the refrigerator. There's no trace of nuts in anything."

"Thank you," I say, my gaze meeting Lucian's.

"You go and get some rest, Miss West," Maggie says. "I'll make some soup for you to eat later." I nod, and she heads to the kitchen.

"Are you ready for that bath, Miss West?"

I take Lucian's hand, and wince in pain when I stand. In a flash, I am scooped up in his arms.

"I can walk. It only hurts a little."

"I know you can. I just want to take care of you."

"Okay."

Lucian carries me into the bathroom, sitting me on the edge of the tub. Filling the tub with water, he adds my favorite bubble bath. The aromatic fragrance of lavender and honey perfumes the air. He lights a few candles, transforming the room into a tranquil spa. Lucian completes the mood by selecting music from my playlist. The first song up is Al Green's, Lets' Stay Together. I stand and undress slowly, never taking my eyes off him. Lucian takes my hand, helping me into the tub.

"Will you join me?"

"Yes, I will," he says, removing his clothes. Lucian climbs in behind me. I'm seated between his long muscular legs. "Lean back."

Submitting to his command, I lean back against his chest. His arms wrap around me, encasing me in his protective embrace. A low groan escapes me. The heated bath and the feel of his skin against mine send ripples of pleasure through me.

"Just relax for a moment. Let the warm water, the candlelight, and the music soothe you."

I submit to the peace and tranquility. I submit to Lucian.

Chapter 6
Lucian

AVERY RELAXES AGAINST my chest, sighing blissfully as the tension leaves her body. I bury my nose in her soft curly strands, kissing her neck. My hand slips down between her thighs, gently nudging them apart.

"Spread your legs." I order, and Avery complies.

She moans and lifts her hips when I stroke her swollen clit. My cock twitches against her backside.

"Tell me what you need?" I whisper in her ear.

"You're all I ever need," she says, but her words are laced with sadness.

"You have me."

"I need all of you, Lucian. I try to ignore the emptiness I feel, but the hunger is insatiable. The need to have you inside me is like an addiction. And cold turkey isn't an option. I love the feel of being totally possessed by you. You've been my obsession for so long, and now that I have you, all I need is you. All I need is your love."

"Turn around and face me," My voice is hoarse, the hunger I feel for her is primal and needy.

Avery turns slowly, straddling me, her beautiful hazel eyes dark pools of lust.

"We'll take it slow; do you understand?"

"Yes." She nods. "We'll take it slow." Leaning forward she covers my mouth with hers. My tongue caresses hers, and she grasps my hair, deepening the kiss.

"Take what you need," I groan into her mouth

I lift her, positioning her so that her cunt hovers above my cock. Avery lowers herself onto me, taking my cock inside her slowly, inch by inch. Her lips part, moaning softly as my cock fills her completely. She rides me slowly, taking what she needs and giving so much more in return. Her beautiful breasts bounce up and down, as her orgasms starts to build.

"You feel so good," she whispers, her moist tongue rimming my ear.

And it blows my fucking mind. All I want is her. Always.

She takes me, grinding slowly, building to an explosive orgasm. Her cunt tightens around my cock, squeezing it, triggering my release. "Avery!" I growl, knowing that she's all I'll ever need. And I'll never let her go.

She rests her forehead on mind. "I love you," she says, her breathing almost back to normal.

"I love you too. Now you need to rest."

I bathe us both quickly, toweling us both dry. I carry Avery into the bedroom and sit her on the edge of the bed. I get her pajamas from her dresser drawer.

"My T-shirt, please," she says.

I know that she feels vulnerable after what happened last night. My old lighthouse T-shirt centers her somehow; it makes her feel connected to me and safe. I grab the T-shirt and white cotton panties.

"Arms up," I order, pulling the shirt down over her head. She steps into her panties next, and I pull them up over her hips. "Get some rest. I'll wake you in a few hours for lunch."

"Will you lay with me until I fall asleep?"

"Of course," I say, dressing myself in sweatpants and a T-shirt.

Avery lies down on the bed and waits for me. She doesn't bother pulling back the bed covers. Climbing in bed behind her, I hold her, my chest to her back. I breathe her in; her scent is heady. She stirs, pressing her hips against my groin. I just had her, but the need to possess her again hardens my cock. I try to focus on anything except the roundness of her ass.

The last thing she needs is me losing control and taking her, the way I've wanted to since she straddled me in my office yesterday. The sound of her breathing evenly lets me know that she's resting peacefully. Untangling our limbs, I climb out of bed, careful not to disturb her.

I make my way to my home office, intending to review the incident report Carter has emailed. A manila envelope on the breakfast bar grabs my attention. Crossing the space in a few long strides, I stop short when I see the name '**Marisa Hunter**' written in bold black letters. The blood in my veins cease flowing and my heart stops for a moment. When I'm finally thinking clearly, I move away from the breakfast bar. I'm running back to the bedroom to assure myself that Avery is still sleeping soundly in our bed. Relieved to find Avery where I left her, I grab my iPhone from the bedside table, before heading back to the breakfast bar.

Making a conference call to Carter and Franklin, I inform them of this new development. Franklin, who resides on the eighth floor, arrives ten minutes after disconnecting the call.

"The envelope was delivered this morning by a bike messenger," Franklin says without preamble.

"Which courier?"

"Zippy Express, Mathers has gone to check it out."

"Good. Carter and his team will be here soon. Other than the messenger, do we know who has handled the package?"

"The messenger left the package with the front desk after he wasn't permitted to deliver it to the penthouse. And Maggie brought it up when she returned with groceries. Including Mack at the front desk, there are three sets of prints that we know of."

After the break-in at Avery's apartment in Chelsea we came clean with Franklin, reminding him of our connection to Avery's past. Behaving a little out of character, he embraced her warmly. Avery returned his hug, thanking him for his part in getting her the help she needed. Franklin released her, but not before giving me a knowing glance.

The day before Camille and I would celebrate our wedding anniversary, I would have a drink with Franklin, and we would toast to the health of Marisa Hunter. Ten years later, I'm a widower in love with the woman formerly known as Marisa Hunter.

"Did you handle the package, sir?" Franklin's question brings me back to the present.

"No, I didn't touch it."

"Has Miss West?"

"No, I haven't told her yet. I need to know more. I don't want anything upsetting her before she has a chance to recover fully."

"I understand," is Franklin's only reply.

Keeping Avery healthy and safe is my number one priority. Telling her about this now will only make matters worse for her recovery. I know this package is another attempt to undermine and intimidate Avery. And before I share this latest piece of information, I want to know everything there is to know. After we questioned the perpetrator, who was responsible for the break-in at Avery's apartment and the lies to the tabloids, all leads have been dead ends. He claims he was just doing his job, proving that there was more to the story. He refuses to give up his source. But it is only a matter of time before we discover who is behind all this.

Chapter 7
Avery

I HEAR FOOTSTEPS APPROACHING before the key enters the lock and the door opens. I know what's coming. Who's coming. The dark shadow enters the small musky room that's been my prison for nearly a month. My body recoils, then stiffens, ready to fight off the inevitable invasion. I've given up praying someone will come to my rescue. My only option is to survive, even when all I want to do is die so the pain will end.

"Are you ready for me, baby girl?"

It's the same question every time, as if anyone is ever ready for pain, humiliation, and captivity.

"How should we start tonight? Should I make you suck my cock and balls first, or should I just fuck you and then make you lick them clean?"

I turn my head away from him, staring at the stained concrete wall.

He laughs sinisterly, ripping away the blanket covering me.

Just breathe, I tell myself.

"Fucking it is then," he taunts, dropping his clothing to the floor as he removes them. "We're going to have a long weekend. No reason why I can't fill every tight little hole you have."

He climbs onto the small bed, making it creak with the extra weight. Fisting his cock with one hand and pressing down on my chest with the other, he rams into me, forcing his way past my resistance. The pain was something I've gotten used to. But I could not control the silent tears that fell. This somehow provoked him, and he pounds harder, causing me to wince and cry out. I fight the screams, trying to hold them back. I know that's what he wants. It's a losing battle; the pain is so unbearable I forget to breathe, and I pray that I never will again.

His grunting always signals the end is near. His hot breath on my neck chills my skin, making my flesh crawl. As much as the penetration pains me, his release repulses me more. The fact that I give him pleasure in any way makes me throw up every time.

"You ready for my seed, baby girl?" he grunts, contaminating my insides, causing a wave of nausea to hit me hard. The weight of his body collapsed on mine, stealing my breath once again.

I'm thankful every day for my birth control implant. Thankful that the choice to get pregnant is still mine to make. His cock shrinks inside me, then falls out of my body. Rolling off me, he laid next to me on his stomach with half his body covering mine. A few moments later, his snoring lets me know he had fallen asleep.

I pray for oblivion, an escape that will free me from this torment. Bound by wrist and ankle restraints, trapped beneath the sadistic warden of this prison. I know freedom will not come tonight.

"Open your eyes Avery, you're safe."

I can hear a voice in the distant calling out to me. But it's too far away. "I'm trapped," I yell out, hoping I'm heard.

"Come back to me." The voice is a gentle whisper and a plea. "You're mine."

"Always," I vow, as my eyes flutters open.

I'm cradled in Lucian's arms, safe from the darkness that waits for me in my nightmares.

He gently wipes away the tears I didn't know were flowing down my cheeks.

"Did I sleepwalk?" I ask once the tears have stopped.

"No, I came into the bedroom, and you were crying in your sleep.

You said you were trapped."

"You told me to come back to you."

"I did," Lucian confirms. "What else did you hear me say?"

"I heard you tell me to open my eyes. You told me I was safe. You said, 'you're mine.' That's what freed me, knowing that I belong with you."

"Always." Lucian echoes my earlier sentiment. "Do you want to talk about your nightmare?"

"It was more of the same. I just want to forget it." Even as I say the words, I know I never will.

"If you're up to it, there's an issue we need to address." I raise my head at the slight hint of concern I hear in Lucian's voice.

"Is there something wrong?" I ask, my own level of worry kicking up a notch.

"I'm not sure. You received a package while you were sleeping."

I raise my eyebrow, questioning why that would be an issue of concern.

"It's addressed to Marisa Hunter," Lucian continues before I voice my thoughts.

"Did you open the package?"

"No, I waited for Carter and his security team to arrive, before coming to wake you."

"I guess I've kept them waiting long enough." Freeing myself from Lucian's hold, I climb out of bed.

"And they can wait a little longer," Lucian says, as he follows me out of bed. Circling me in his arms, pressing my back to his chest, Lucian inhales deeply. "I want to make sure you're alright before we take another step."

"I'm okay," I tell him, but we both know it's a lie. I'm far from okay. In the past 24 hours, someone has tried to kill me, which I'm sure triggered my anxiety, causing a nightmare. Now there's a package addressed to the girl I used to be. The girl who was sold, abandoned, raped, and tortured. The girl I tried to bury ten years ago. But sure, I'm okay.

"You don't need to pretend with me. I know how fucked up this is, but whatever comes we face it together."

After a moment of silence, when I offer no response, Lucian turns me around to face him. His intense blue irises meet my teary hazel gaze. Pulling me against his chest, Lucian holds me while I break down, sobbing like a child.

"I'm fine really," I say ironically, after the last tear is shed. "I need to get dress."

Lucian gives me a chaste kiss before releasing me. I watch him remove his T-shirt, wet with my tears, replacing it with another. After I've dressed in yoga pants and a fitted T-shirt, Lucian takes my hand, leading me out of the bedroom.

Lucian's security team focus on us as we enter the living room. I immediately notice the manila envelope on the breakfast bar and my step falters a bit. Lucian squeezes my hand, offering reassurance.

"We need you to open the envelope so that we can examine the contents." Carter's rich baritone voice is the first to speak.

I nod, lifting the envelope and opening it, dropping the contents on the breakfast bar. There is a sheet of plain white paper and a photo of Lucian and I, leaving the hospital earlier today. I shudder, the sight chilling me to the bone. Lucian wraps his arm around me, pulling me close to his side, before turning the paper over to reveal what's written on it.

I tried to warn you, to give you a chance to do the right thing. Next time I will be more direct. I will expose the truth and watch as the lies destroy you.

I don't know if it's a warning, a threat, or both. But fear races through me like a champion thoroughbred. I try to think of anyone who might want to hurt me, and I come up blank. Living like a recluse for the past ten years, you tend not to make any enemies. It's only recently that my world has expanded to include Lucian. All this drama began when Lucian and I started dating. There has been a series of events. My apartment was broken into, and then there was the incident with the tabloids. Someone is deliberately trying to frighten me or worse. Causing me to go into anaphylactic shock is a clear indication that this person doesn't care if I live or die. Who would do such a thing and why? Memories of my encounters with Samantha and all the things she said to me come flooding back all at once.

It's not our time. I will wait for him to come to his senses, because I'm the one he's meant to be with.

"It's Samantha." My voice is barely audible.

"Samantha who?" Carter queries.

"Samantha Davies," Lucian provides. "My sister-in-law."

"She's obsessed with Lucian, and she believes that it's only a matter of time before they're together." Lucian, Carter, and Franklin listen as I recount my run-ins with Samantha.

"That's not proof of her guilt, but it's a place to start," Carter assures. "If there's a connection I'll find it," he adds, before sending a text.

A few moments later, a young woman arrives carrying a case with the words Thorne Security displayed on it. She retrieves a large plastic evidence bag from the case after passing Carter a single rubber glove.

"I need to take these items; there may be usable prints on them." Carter places the photo, the note, and the envelope in the evidence bag. The woman seals the bag and leaves without uttering a word.

Releasing his hold on me, Lucian walks Carter to the elevator. I take a seat, curling my legs up on the couch. Franklin hovers nearby keeping a watchful eye on me. The stress of recent events has me physically and mentally drained. My eyelids are heavy as my head flops down, resting on the armrest of the couch. Softness surrounds me. I snuggle into the warmth, drifting off to sleep.

I'm still curled up on the couch when I awake to the most appetizing aromas. My stomach growls, reminding me that it's been hours since I last ate. With a pressing need to pee, I remove the blanket covering me and hurry to the bathroom. After relieving myself, I wash my hands and freshen up a bit before joining Lucian in the kitchen.

Approaching the kitchen, the warmth of his gaze is inviting. He takes me in from head to toe, before striding up to me. Lucian pulls me to his chest, holding me close in his arms.

"Did you sleep well?"

I nod. "All my dreams were of you." I can feel his smile against my hair.

"Are you hungry?"

"Very," I say, tilting my head to meet his gaze. "But we should probably have some food first."

Lucian takes a deep breath, his lips part slightly, and his eyes are dark with desire. His reaction heats my core and dampens my panties. I love that he doesn't try to hide how I affect him. And I love that he craves me as much as I crave him.

Because it's been too long since we shared a real kiss, I rise on my tiptoes covering his mouth with mine. The kiss is soft and loving at first, then it morphs into something more primal and aggressive. Lucian's arms tighten around my waist, lifting me off my feet. In two long strides, Lucian pins me against the wall. I wrap my legs around his waist, crushing my mouth to his, singeing my lips with the heat of our kiss.

Lucian breaks the kiss, gliding his lips down my neck. He adjusts his hold on me to suck and bite my nipples through my T-shirt. The pain and pleasure blaze a trail from my nipples directly to my throbbing pussy. Seeking more, I arch into him, silently begging him to never stop.

When my breathing becomes uneven, Lucian stops instantly.

"Please don't stop. I want you," I pant.

Lucian press his lips to my forehead, before resting his head on mine and closing his eyes. We stay like that until I'm breathing easy again.

"If anything happened to you, I wouldn't survive it. Let me take care of you, Sweetness." Lucian opens his eyes, before planting me firmly on my feet. “Behave and I promise to fuck you senseless the moment you’re all better.”

“I’m going to hold you to that promise, Mr. Thorne.”

“I’m looking forward to it.”

Leading me to the breakfast bar, Lucian serves me a meal of creamy chicken pot pie soup and baguettes. It’s the most delicious soup I’ve ever had. We eat in silence, enjoying each other’s company without feeling the need to converse. After our meal, I insist on helping Lucian with the dishes.

We settle on the couch for a quiet evening in. I grab my copy of Jane Eyre from the coffee table to read, and Lucian is reading over reports. I realize I’ve been staring at Lucian, after I have read the same paragraph five times. I’m captivated by my man, the way his lips curl slightly when he knows I’m watching him. The way his intense blue eyes dance with excitement. And the crooked smile that melts my panties every time.

“I was thinking we could leave a day early. Relax a little on the beach before the celebrating begins.”

Lucian’s parents’ wedding anniversary party is a week away. The weekend will be filled with all types of festivities celebrating their thirty years of marriage. The itinerary includes a family dinner on Friday, the main event Saturday night, and the celebration ends with brunch on Sunday. I’m also hoping Lucian and I can squeeze in a visit to the Montauk Lighthouse.

“The follow-up appointment with my doctor is on Thursday at eleven-thirty. We can leave any time after that.”

“It’s settled then. After your appointment, we’ll have lunch together before leaving for the beach house.

Abandoning his attempt to work, Lucian and I decide to watch a movie. I lay down with my head resting on his lap, my wavy locks covering his thighs.

Lucian combs his fingers through my hair, massaging my scalp, relaxing me and taking away the stress that's been clinging to me. His touch soothes me, releasing the tension that has me in knots.

"That feels good," I say. "Your magic fingers are just what the doctor orders."

"If you think this feels good, wait until I get my hands on the rest of you."

"I promised to behave, so that means you have to as well."

"Any other time I'd love to have you tied in knots, with silk ropes in all the right places. But tonight, all I'm offering is a massage."

I gasp, understanding his meaning. He has restrained me with handcuffs, silk ties, and scarves. The thought of being bound with ropes for him frightens me, but it also excites me more than it should, which is why I'm surprised when I hear myself say, "I think I'd like to try that."

I can feel Lucian's cock growing harder near my head. "Soon, Rose Pedal," he moans. And I know it's a promise he intends to keep.

Chapter 8
Lucian

I RETURNED TO WORK on Monday morning and over the next several days Avery and I fall into a comfortable routine. Dinner together every evening, followed by some downtime either reading or watching television for a couple of hours. Each night we find new ways to be intimate without making love, sensual kisses, gentle massages, and a relaxing soak in the tub. Do I miss being buried deep inside her? Hell yes. But her health is more important, and she is worth waiting for. After her doctor's appointment Avery will be joining me for lunch in Bryant Park.

Standing at the entrance of Bryant Park Grill, the ivy-covered restaurant seems out of place. Surrounded by the soaring skyscrapers in the heart of the city, it feels like it belongs in another world.

Awareness heats my skin, sending an electric charge through me. I sense Avery before I see her coming up the steps into Bryant Park. The park is filled by a host of people enjoying the clear summer day. But I am deaf and blind to all the distractions. She has my full attention. When she is finally in the shelter of my arms, pressing her lips to mine, I feel whole again. No one else matters when the woman I love kisses me so passionately it makes me weak in the knees. Kissing her did that to me every goddamn time. A wrecking ball couldn't devastate me more.

We have our lunch on the rooftop terrace. Taking in the scenery below us, we enjoy a meal of Wild Mushroom Ravioli, with a glass of Pinot Noir.

As much as I'm looking forward to spending time with my family and friends, I'm desperate to claim Avery again, to be deep inside, filling her utterly. My dick twitches at the image of her beneath me. I want to hear her screaming my name again and again, until we are too exhausted to move.

I pay the check and we make our way out of the park. Hand in hand, we walk the short distance to the limo, where our bags are already loaded for the ride to my beach house.

Avery suddenly stops. Looking over her shoulder, she quickly scans the faces of a few pedestrians.

"What is it?" I ask when her hand become ice cold in mine.

Facing me, she tries to hide the fear clearly visible in her hazel irises.

"It's nothing... I..." Avery clears her throat before beginning again. "For a moment, it felt like we were being followed."

I look back and see Mathers flanked by two additional security personnel.

"It's just your security detail." I point Mathers out to her. Sighing, Avery nods, giving me a reassuring smile that doesn't quite reach her eyes.

We approach the limo and Franklin opens the back-passenger door. Sliding across the seat Avery peers out the window. I climb in beside her, noticing she hasn't stopped shivering. I pull her onto my lap. She comes willingly, snuggling close, my body heat warming her. I know the uneasiness Avery is feeling has everything to do with her suspicions about Samantha. Someone is obviously following us. How else do you explain the note and the photo of Avery and I leaving the hospital? Carter began investigating Samantha right away, but so far, he has found nothing. Either she's innocent or much clever than anyone has given her credit for.

"Feeling better?" I ask, after we've left the city.

"Much better." Avery lifts her head, meeting my gaze. "It gets to me sometimes, knowing that someone is watching me. How can I protect myself when I can't see the threat coming?"

"Thorne Security has Samantha under surveillance. We know where she is twenty-four-seven. Everyone she interacts with is treated as a suspect, and they will be investigated as a potential accomplice. I won't let anything happen to you. No one will ever hurt you again."

Avery rests her forehead against mine briefly, before sliding off my lap and taking a seat beside me.

"My doctor has given me a clean bill of health. She assures me that it's perfectly safe to engage in my regular physical activities." This time Avery's smile reaches her eyes and it's brighter than the sun.

"Did she now?" I can't stop myself from matching her smile.

I haven't fucked Avery in five days and the absence of her sweet cunt has me feeling a little irritable. This morning I was tempted to jerk off in the shower. But the thought of my seed not being inside her stopped me. I can see she needs this connection as much as I do. The thought of her wet pussy strangling my cock has it pressing painfully against my zipper. Tonight, we will get what we so desperately crave. I want to be covered in the scent of her essence, from sunset to sunrise.

A few hours later Franklin is pulling up the driveway of my beach house. Avery is sound asleep, resting her head on my lap.

"Sweetness." Stroking her cheek, I coax her awake. "Wake up, sleeping beauty."

She stirs, her eyes fluttering open briefly, before nuzzling her cheek against my crotch. "Five more minutes and I'm all yours," she murmurs.

I lift her up into my arms, ignoring my now-hard cock. "We've arrived," I whisper, pressing my lips to her ear.

Opening her eyes, Avery leans back to meet my gaze.

"I had the most wonderful dream," she beams.

"What did you dream about?" I ask when sadness replace the joy on her face.

Avery is silent for long seconds before she speaks again.

"I was dreaming about my wedding." She pauses, lowering her eyes as if the confession is something to be ashamed of.

"Why has that made you sad?"

"My parents were there, and I know that can never be. My father will never walk me down the aisle or give me away. And my mother will never help me find the perfect dress."

"If there was anything, I could do to give you that on our wedding day, I would."

The gravity of my words has my heart pounding in my chest. Not because I'm afraid, but because I know deep in my soul that this woman will be my wife someday soon.

"Our wedding?" Avery whispers, her voice barely audible.

"You will walk down the aisle to me and only me."

"Yes, I will."

We can't deny the bond fate has created between us. Sharing a kiss, we know it's a prelude to what's to come.

Avery slips her sandals back on and we climb out of the limo. The ocean breeze welcomes me with a gentle kiss. Taking Avery's hand in mine, we make our way up the steps of our home for the next few days. Franklin follows closely with our bags.

Approaching the porch, the memory of Avery sitting on the swing drinking lemonade curls my lips upward in a smile. I'm also reminded how Avery was convinced that the beach house had appeared in a television series. '*You know the one with the girl who has the same last name as you?*' she said all those weeks ago.

I look at Avery and my heart skips a beat when I see the love reflected in her hazel eyes. A hint of sadness lingers, and I want nothing more than to chase it away. Leaning down, I kiss her forehead, before planting a kiss on her lips.

The door is unlocked, thanks to my parent's housekeeper coming by to air the place out and stock a few groceries. We walk inside, and I instruct Franklin to leave the bags near the door.

"We can manage from here, Franklin. Go and enjoy your time off." Although he is off for the next few days he will be staying locally in a hotel, in case of an emergency.

"Yes sir," he says, leaving after he has said goodbye to Avery.

"It's just you and me now for the next 24-hours," I announce, after Franklin leaves and closes the door.

"Whatever shall we do with the time?" Avery, feigning innocent, has me stalking after her when she turns to run up the stairs.

I catch up to her in two long strides. Scooping her up into my arms, I carry her to the master bedroom

"We're not leaving this bed until I forget how much I miss burying my cock deep inside your sweet cunt."

Avery shudders in my arms. Her body's reaction to my declaration sends a surge of lust coursing through me. My lips go to her throat, brushing gently against her soft skin.

"Lucian..." she pants. Her lips are slightly parted and her eyelids heavy with desire.

"I'm going to take care of you, but for now let me have you the way I want you."

She shudders again. "Yes."

In a few quick steps I have her on the bed, beneath me. My mouth finds hers; the kiss is soft and warm at first, her tongue circling mine. My hands go to the sides of her head, holding her still. Fisting her hair, the kiss becomes hot and demanding. The thirst I have for her, needs to be quenched desperately. Moving down her body, I push her dress up. Her flat belly invites me to kiss it. Laying between her legs, I pull her panties to the side, and my tongue glides over her throbbing clit.

Avery cries out, her hips jerking up presses against my mouth. She moves frantically seeking more friction. I torment and pleasure her with my mouth, nipping and sucking at her hungrily.

"Come for me my rose petal," I urge her before my tongue flutters against her swollen clit.

She screams my name through an explosive orgasm. Her sweet essence covers my lips and chin. "You taste so good."

She moans when I emphasize by licking between her slick folds.

Leaning back on my haunches, I loosen my belt, unzip my pants, and push them down past my hips, freeing my cock

Avery reaches for me. "Hurry," she pleas. Lifting her legs, I remove her panties and she spreads them wide for me.

"Raise your hands above your head," I command gently.

Without being told she grabs hold of the headboard. Her submission is a gift to be cherished. My mouth waters at the sight of her open for me to do with as I please. I lean forward, supporting my weight on my elbow. Hovering above her, my lips are a breath away from hers. I can feel her heart racing with anticipation. With my free hand, I guide my cock into her tight wet cunt. Pushing deep, I stretch her inch by inch, until I fill her completely.

I close my eyes, holding still inside her, fighting for control. Biting down on my lower lip, I allow the pain to center me.

"I don't know if I can be gentle," I confess, resting my forehead on hers. "You feel so good, and I've missed you so fucking much."

Wrapping her legs around me, Avery pleas, "Just fuck me, Lucian."

I pull my cock out halfway before pounding into her. She cries out as her pussy tightens around me, strangling my cock, and the sensation is phenomenal.

Her lips brush against mine. "I've missed you too," she moans into my mouth.

God, I love her.

Thrust after thrust, I drive into her. A primal grunt escapes each time I hit the end of her. I want this to last, but the need to fill her with my seed overwhelms me. And when the sweetest pussy I've ever had squeezes my dick so goddam tight, I almost lose it.

"Fuck," I groan. "That's it, squeeze my cock. Make me come, Rose Petal."

Each thrust buries me deeper inside Avery, hitting her G-spot again and again. Her back arches as another orgasm shatters her utterly. Unbearable pleasure races up my spine, drawing my balls up, thickening and lengthening my cock. My release is near.

Growling like an animal and throwing my head back, I spurt into her. Holding Avery's body tight against mine, I pound into her, releasing my seed, coming long and hard. My semen fills her until it flows from her sweet pussy, slicking her inner thighs.

Her arms wrap around my back, holding me tight as my hips slowly stop grinding. My soft cock is still inside her and I make no attempt to pull out.

After a few moments, I rise up, balancing the weight of my body on my elbows. Burying my face in her neck, I brush my lips over her ear and whisper, "I'm not done with you yet. We have more orgasms to make up for."

Lifting her hips, she moans. My cock stiffens and we start again.

Chapter 9
Avery

THE GLARE FROM THE sun peeking through the curtains wakes me. Rolling over, I expect to find Lucian fast asleep beside me. The absence of him has me climbing out of bed and picking up his shirt from the floor. I put it on, buttoning it as I pad barefoot through the beach house in search of him.

I make my way to the kitchen. Although he is no longer here, there is evidence that he recently was. A fresh pot of coffee awaits me, along with a note that reads.

Gone for a swim.

I make myself a cup of coffee before heading to the pool, only to discover that Lucian is not there either. I decide to stop searching and let him come to me. The front porch is where I choose to wait for him. From the swing, I have a perfect view of the ocean. That's when I notice movement against the ocean currents, and I know it's Lucian. He has gone for a swim in the Atlantic. I'm down the steps and walking toward the beach before I realize it. Sitting on the sand, I watch him swim to the buoy, his powerful strokes bringing him back effortlessly.

When Lucian emerges from the water, his body glistens under the morning sun. A sight to behold. A gift from Poseidon. He's the most beautiful sea creature I've ever seen. And he's all mine.

I know the moment he sees me, his long strides falters. I smile, loving the effect I have on him. The nearness of him has the same effect on me. My pulse quickens, racing my heart, causing me to be nearly breathless with anticipation.

Standing before me soaking wet, he looks down at me. His bare chest glistens with ocean water, and his swim trunks clings to him, hanging low on his hips, showing off his lean muscles and spectacular abs. However, it's his bulging cock I can't tear my eyes away from, made even more visible by the wetness of his swim trunks. Dropping to his knees, Lucian leans in to give me a kiss.

"Good morning, beautiful." His smile is followed by another kiss.

"It most certainly is," I quip. "The view is amazing." I glare at his cock once again.

"Do you see something you like?" Meeting his gaze, I lick my lips, wanting to taste him.

"No."

Lucian frowns, questioning me silently.

"It's beyond like. I see something I crave. Something that has me addicted. Something I know is mine."

A well of emotions are visible in the intense gaze of his blue irises that rivals the Caribbean Ocean.

"I fucking love you, woman," he groans, pinning me down in the sand. The wetness from his body and swim trunks dampens the shirt I'm wearing.

"You're wet," I giggle when the water from his hair trickles down to my cheek.

"Are you wet?" Lucian asks, a wicked smile curls his lips.

Lowering his head, Lucian kisses me, nipping at my bottom lip. I'm not too worried about onlookers. The area near Lucian's beach house has us sheltered from prying eyes. The freedom makes me bold. Tangling my legs with his, I roll until he is beneath me. Reclaiming his lips, I plunge my tongue into his mouth. His hands fist my hair, keeping me still. Our teeth and tongues collide in a desperate attempt to devour each other.

I don't try to understand the visceral reaction I have to him. The way my body is so attuned to his. How the thought of him filling me sends indescribable pleasure coursing through me. The need to have him satiate the ache deep inside me grows with every kiss and every touch, becoming unbearable. I know it's the same for him. I can feel the tension in his body beneath me; the way his hands are gripping my hips and the harshness of his breathing. He's working hard to yield control to me, which makes me crave him more.

A wild and desperate need drives me, forcing me to let go of any remaining inhibitions. Fumbling with the waistband of his swim trunks, I attempt to free his cock. Lucian's hand covers mine, stopping me.

"Is this what you want, Avery?" he groans. "To take me here, where anyone can see us."

I never thought much about exhibitionism, but I can't deny the wickedly intense pleasure it elicits in me. I writhe against his cock, imagining the possession, taking him into my body. Showing the world he's mine.

"I want you."

"You have me."

"I want you right now."

"But, why here, Avery?"

"Because... I..." My resolve falters a bit. "Because you're mine and I don't care who knows it."

Releasing my hand, Lucian urges, "Take what you want, Rose Petal. Take what's yours." His fiery gaze heats me from the inside out. "Fill your greedy little cunt with me."

My fingers glide under the waistband of his swim trunk, stroking his cock. I rub my thumb on the head of his cock, wiping away the pre-cum that has leaked out. Lucian's thrust against my hand, and the low growl deep in his throat, sounds primal, almost animalistic. Releasing his cock, I bring my thumb to my mouth, sucking it clean.

"You taste so good." Repeating his words, I lick my lips for effect.

"Fuck me." The words are almost inaudible. But I hear them clearly. Feel the need in his taut body. See the love in his blue eyes staring back at me.

"I intend to."

Lucian's hands slide under the shirt I'm wearing. When his hands grip my bare hips, his cock grows harder beneath me.

"You're not wearing any panties," he hisses

I shake my head, then take him in my hand guiding his cock to my center. I'm so wet for him the glide down his thick large cock is made easier. Inch by inch I cover him. The pain of stretching morphs into pleasure. Pleasure so profound a single tear trickles down my cheek. With one upward thrust Lucian is buried deep inside me. I want to go slow, take my time and enjoy the feel of him, to savor him. But Lucian has other plans. He grips my hips, lift me up, and lower me down, plowing deep into me.

I bite my bottom lip to keep from crying out, as unfathomable pleasure pushes me over the edge so fast, my body trembles, then shatters into a million pieces. Lucian doesn't give me time to recover. He lifts and lowers me again and again, hitting the sweetest spot known to man. Clenching tightly around him, tension starts to build in me again.

Leaning down, I give him a deep kiss.

"Come for me, Lucian." I moan against his lips.

He groans and something inside him is set free. Something desperate and needy, filling me with a long deep thrust. My nails dig into his shoulders, marking his skin even as I cover his cock with my essence. His rhythm is faster, racing to completion. I match his pace, chasing my own release. My body clamoring to have his seed inside me.

Shaking violently, my pussy tightens around Lucian's cock, squeezing it so hard, I think I might break it.

Heaven knows that would be a shameful waste of manhood.

"Oh, god... Lucian... it feels so good." My voice is so raspy I barely recognize it.

Lucian's body quakes beneath me; the magnitude of his orgasm is off the Richter Scale. A warm sensation floods me, triggering my own release. Together we plunge over the edge, tethered to each other.

I don't know how long it takes my body to relax, or for Lucian's cock to stop twitching inside me. Laying on top of him, I could die at this moment, and I'd be a happy woman, because loving Lucian and being loved by him, life doesn't get any better.

When Lucian's cock softens and falls from my body, he sits up, holding me close to his chest.

"Let's go inside and get cleaned up," he says, standing as I cling to him with my arms and legs cocooning his body.

After we have showered and dressed, we make our way to the kitchen for much needed sustenance. Fresh croissants, delicious berries, and Greek yogurt. Lucian insists on making Mimosas, which have a lot more champagne than orange juice.

We spend the afternoon relaxing on the deck and laying in the sun. Whether we are splashing around in the pool or napping on a lounge chair big enough for two, we're in each other's arms. But the absolute best part about spending the day in the sun with Lucian is without a doubt, suntan lotion.

His fingers massage the lotion into my skin, covering my body. Strong hands move over my shoulders, down my arms and back, along the length of my spine, kneading my hips and thighs. When he urges me to turn over onto my back, my nipples peak, eager for his touch. I moan when his thumb glides over them making them harder. Lucian smiles, fully aware of what he's doing to me and pleased with my response. Moving down to my abdomen, and around my waist, he lingers between my thighs. He gives my feet special attention, rubbing my soles, hitting the pressure points. It feels almost as good as an orgasm.

By the time he's done, I'm purring. Every muscle in my body is blissfully relaxed. And the only thing on my mind is returning the favor. I can't wait to get my hands on his body.

God, I love this man.

• • • •

WHEN EVENING COMES, we head out to meet everyone for the family dinner. Lucian is dressed in a casual linen suit. I've chosen to wear a silky floral dress with strappy high heel sandals. My neck is adorned with a strand of pearls, a gift from

Lucian. He says it's a belated birthday present. They are gorgeous and very long, hanging well past my belly button. I have layered them, creating a multi-strand look.

We step out into the evening air, and the ocean breeze whispers seductively, promising a memorable night. Lucian opens the passenger door of his Mercedes AMG GT, helping me inside and securing my seatbelt before shutting the door. I watch as he rounds the front of the vehicle and climb into the driver's seat.

Arriving at the restaurant, the valet parks the car, and we head inside where we are greeted by an enthusiastic hostess.

"Welcome back, Mr. Thorne," she says, unable to take her eyes off Lucian to acknowledge that he's not alone. "Let me show you to the private dining room your parents have reserved."

"Thank you," Lucian replies.

We follow her, and I watch as the sway of her hips become exaggerated. Tossing her straight black hair over her shoulder, she looks back to ask, "Will you be visiting long?"

Before Lucian can get a word out, I find myself responding.

"We're here for the weekend. We'll be heading back to the city Sunday evening."

That got her attention. She rakes her eyes over me as if seeing me for the first time. When her gaze travels to our joined hands, I think she gets the message. She continues without saying another word until we reach the entrance of the private dining room.

"Enjoy your night," she murmurs.

I can't hold back the next two words that pass my lips.

"We will."

Lucian gives my hand a gentle squeeze, then lifts our entwined hands, pressing his lips against my knuckles.

"I love it when you're territorial," he says, loud enough for my ears only.

Clasping his hand tighter, I whisper, "Mine."

"Always," he vows.

We enter the private dining room, and the hostess scampers off. My eyes are immediately drawn to the massive chandelier shimmering in the center of the ceiling. The dining room is beautifully decorated. There are two tables, seating ten each. The tables are covered with crisp white linen and adorned with crystal glasses, linen napkins, and sparkling silverware. But the centerpiece is the showstopper. A candelabra sits in the center of each table, surrounded by an elegant wreath of white roses and orchids. The fragrance of the bouquets fills the room. The atmosphere is warm and inviting, yet intimate despite the number of guests.

A white-jacket server greets us, carrying a tray with flutes filled with champagne. Lucian takes two glasses, offering one to me.

"Let's go say hello to my parents," Lucian says, leading the way.

Lucinda beams when she sees her son approaching. I hadn't noticed until now how much Lucian resembles his mother. They share the same dark hair and that same crooked smile I love. Her eyes are brown, whereas his are a vibrant blue. The same as his biological father.

"Hello, sweethearts." She extends both her hands. Lucian and I reach for her, each taking an offered hand.

Kissing us both on the cheek, she leans in for a group hug. Now I know where Katelyn gets it from. They're both huggers. "It's good to see you both."

"It's good to see you too," Lucian and I say in unison.

Stepping out of our embrace, she smiles at us with such happiness, it's written all over her face.

We're joined by Charles, who greets us with equal joy. Resting his hand at his wife's lower back, he urges Lucian to introduce me to his grandparents.

Seated at what I refer to as table one are Charles' parents. Alexander and Kathleen Thorne, who recently celebrated sixty-five years of marriage by taking a transatlantic cruise. Lucinda's mother Alice Daly-Moore and her sister Julia Frost are seated at her right and left respectively. Alice remarried two years ago, after being widowed for fifteen years. Her new husband, John Moore, sits next to her. Julia is here with Paulo, her much younger Italian companion. I'm not clear what their relationship status is. According to her mother, "he's something she picked up in Brazil last month." I try to hold back my giggles when she whispers that bit of information in my ear. Rounding out the group are my surrogate parents, Conrad and Evelyn Preston.

Since meeting the Thornes, I've learned they have been acquainted with the Prestons for years. Lucinda even met my mom once. Hearing that caused me to breakdown. This new revelation coming the day after I found out that Lucian's biological father is the same man who adopted me and then sold me to pay off a gambling debt. Lucinda held me when uncontrollable sobs quaked my body. Soothing me as only a mother could. Standing in for the mother I lost and the mother who was miles away.

"Avery, dear, are you alright?" Evelyn's voice pulls me off the road to melancholy lane.

"I'm fine," I say, leaning in to kiss her cheek.

"Are you sure?"

"Perfectly," I assure her as I give Conrad a quick peck on his cheek.

Lucian has escaped his grandparents and is standing beside me exchanging greetings with the Prestons.

"Shall we find our seats?" he asks, after promising Evelyn a dance.

With his hand resting possessively at the small of my back, Lucian maneuvers us effortlessly around the servers, carrying champagne and hors d'oeuvres. Our table has mostly familiar faces. However, there are two new faces. A man, one of the unknown faces, springs from his chair, grabbing Lucian in a bear hug. A few seconds of male bonding and back slapping later they separate.

"Long time no see, Luci," the man says, smiling mischievously.

Lucian's smile is just as playful when he turns to face me. Taking my hand, he introduces me to the man who looks remarkably like his aunt Julia.

"I would like you to meet my cousin, Julian Frost. He then turns to Julian, and says, "Julian this is my girlfriend, Avery West."

I extend my hand to shake Julian's, but he lifts it to his mouth, kissing it before releasing it.

"It's a pleasure to meet you, Avery." He winks, nodding his head towards Lucian. "Anytime you get bored with this one, give me a call."

I step back, wrapping my arm around Lucian's waist. "That time doesn't exist," I scowl, upset by his manner of joking.

He chuckles, clearly not offended by my response. "I like her," he says pointedly to Lucian.

"I like her too," Lucian shares before pressing his lips against my hair.

"Come," Julian urges. "Meet my little sister."

A striking blonde stands when Julian extends his hand to her. She's the most ethereal woman I have ever seen. With pale skin, platinum blonde hair flowing down her back, and icy blue eyes, she is beautiful and almost unreal. Her eyes are the same as her brother's. Aside from that there is little resemblance.

We take our seats at the table. Lucian and his brother Daniel sits at the head of the table on opposite ends. I take the seat at Lucian's right, and Julian is at his left with sister Olivia next to him. Jake is next to her, and Raina is beside him. But the person I'm most surprised to see is Chris, sitting at Daniel's right. Marcus and Katelyn complete our group.

The conversation ebbs and flows among our dinner companions. Jake's wicked sense of humor has everyone in stitches. I don't think I've ever laughed so hard. I can see what Raina sees in him. He's witty, charming, and extremely good looking. And he's crazy about my best friend.

The servers move about the room, refilling glasses before they are empty. Dinner is a seven-course meal, with everything superbly prepared. We've barely finished the main course, before the servers are removing the plates only to be replaced with another equally appetizing dish.

After dinner, everyone begins socializing, moving from table to table. Lucian has stepped away to speak with Daniel and I take the opportunity to catch up with Chris. We're on the dance floor while our men have a chat.

"I'm surprised to see you here," I tell Chris, during a slow dance. "The last time we spoke Daniel hadn't come out yet." I keep my voice low, so I'm not overheard. "Has that changed?"

"No, but he intends to tell his family after the anniversary celebration."

"That's great, I'm..." I cut myself off.

"What is it?" he asks.

"Nothing, it's just I think Lucian may have already put two and two together. He observed you and Daniel at his fundraiser dinner last month. He asked me who you're dating. He knows you're gay."

Chris nods, absorbing all I've said.

"He hasn't said anything to Daniel." Chris looks over at the brothers engaged in deep conversation. "If he had, Daniel would have told me," Chris adds.

"He wouldn't, that's not his style. He wouldn't 'out' his brother or anyone for that matter. It's not his secret to tell," I assure Chris.

The song ends, and Chris lead me back to the table. We're joined by Katelyn and Raina.

"My feet are killing me," Raina complains. "I love dancing, but Jake seems to never run out of energy."

"He's always been the life of the party," Katelyn says, staring at the dance floor where Marcus is holding Olivia.

Katelyn and I have gotten close during the last few weeks. And I know we have a long way to go before we are sharing all our secrets. But I recognize the yearning in her eyes and the sadness in her voice. She's in love with Marcus.

"My mom can have the next couple dances, while I rest my feet." Raina's comment brings my attention to Evelyn and Jake on the dance floor.

The Twist by Chubby Checker has almost everyone returning to the dance floor.

I grab Katelyn's hand, pulling her up from her seat. "Come on," I plea, wanting to cheer her up.

"What the hell." she concedes.

"Wait for me," Raina says, following close behind.

The three of us dance and giggle for the next five songs. On the last song Katelyn grabs Olivia's hand as she walks by, including her cousin in our dance. When the music changes to a slow tempo, we leave the dance floor together. I'm about to take my seat when strong possessive fingers wrap around my wrist.

"It's my turn." There's no mistaking the need in Lucian's voice. The need to hold me. The need to claim me. The need to love me.

Leading me to the dance floor, he holds me close. Our bodies move in sync to Etta James' At Last. The lyrics of the song speaks to the essence of our love, casting a spell over us. Lucian's lips brushes against my ear, as he serenades me. By the time he croons the lyrics, *for you are mine, at last*. I'm pressing my thighs together to alleviate the ache.

"How are you feeling, Sweetness?" He whispers, fully aware of the fire he has lit inside me

To take my mind off the incessant throbbing at my center, I ask a question of my own.

"Has Alexander always been your middle name or did your parents change it when Charles adopted you?"

He chuckles at my attempt at distraction.

"Alexander is the middle name given to me at birth by my mother. It's a middle name my father, Daniel, and I share. It was also my son's middle name," he says with a heavy sigh, and I know it's due to the memory of his late son. "It's in honor of my grandfather."

"It's a strong name, it means defender of men. You're a born protector. Your son would have been proud of you."

Lucian holds me, swaying through two more songs. The last being Michael Bublé's Save the Last Dance for Me. The lyrics deliver a warning and a promise. When the song ends, we make our way to our seats. The servers have cleared the tables of everything except the centerpieces. The clinking of metal against crystal has everyone's attention on Charles.

"I'd like to thank you all for coming out tonight, for sharing in our celebration." He reaches out to Lucinda, and she takes his hand, standing by his side as he speaks to their family and friends. "I can't believe that it's been thirty years since this beautiful woman agreed to blend our lives, sharing everything, including our sons. Blended families often go through a transitional phase. Everyone trying to figure out where they belong. But my loving wife made our family whole from day one. Choosing this woman as the mother of our children was the second-best decision I've ever made. Becoming her husband was the first." He kisses her tenderly on the forehead, before asking everyone to stand. "To the only woman I have eyes for, thank you for thirty amazing years." We raise our champagne flute with him, honoring his wife.

Lucian's grandparents left after the toast. And nearly an hour later we're navigating the room saying goodnight to everyone in attendance. We're leaving the restaurant when we spot Julian. He's ushering the enthusiastic hostess who greeted us earlier into the back of a Bentley.

"Good night, Luci." He waves. "See you tomorrow, Avery," he says, as he climbs into the car.

Once we're on the road a few minutes, I ask the question that's been eating at me all night.

"Why does Julian call you Luci?"

"For the same reason I call him Julie."

"Because you were both named after your moms?"

"We are, but that's not why."

"Care to enlighten me?"

Lucian clears his throat before he begins with the tale of Luci and Julie.

"For the first few years of his life, Julian stuttered badly. He could barely get my name out. Whenever I went for a visit with my aunt Julia and my uncle Jeremy."

"Julian's father," I interrupt.

"Yes," he confirms. "Jeremy Frost owns a massive estate in Upstate New York called Frost Haven. "So, to make me feel better, he told me to call him Julie. Now he does it just to remind himself of a different time."

"Are you two still close?"

"Very. We've done a lot of business together over the years."

"What does he do?"

"He's a real estate developer."

"He seems lost to me, like he's missing something."

"You're very observant, Sweetness. But that's a story for another time."

The car comes to a stop in the driveway of Lucian's beach house. The moon casts a glow over the ocean, inviting me in for a swim. Lucian scoops me up in his arms and carries me up the steps, making his intentions clear.

I wrap my arms around his neck, snuggling against his chest.

"I love you, Mr. Thorne."

"I love you too, Miss West."

It's been a long night and I should feel weary, yet somehow, I feel invigorated. I know I owe the surge of energy to the man holding me. I know that whatever he has planned for us tonight will be amazing.

We enter the house and Lucian carries me directly to the bedroom.

"Did you have a good time tonight, my rose petal?"

"Yes, I did. I especially enjoyed meeting your grandparents.

"And they enjoyed meeting you." Brushing his lips gently against my ear, he whispers, "You were beautiful on the dance floor tonight. I couldn't take my eyes off you."

"I felt you watching me," I confess.

"I wanted you to feel me. To feel me touching you, even when I'm across the room."

"You made me feel desired. And I wanted to show you how much your touch means to me."

"Is that why you were so enticing. You wanted me to dance with you?"

"No, I was dancing for you. Every pulsing beat, every sway of my hips was for you."

Lucian covers my mouth, singeing my lips and melting my panties. It's been too long since he last kissed me. Too long since being breathless meant I was truly alive.

I fucking love this man.

Entering the bedroom, Lucian plants me firmly on my feet, before shutting the door behind us. I'm undressing when his words render me motionless. It takes my brain a moment to process what he's saying.

"I want you to strip for me, then I want a lap dance," he says, pulling the chair away from the desk to take a seat. "I want a private show."

His simple commands travel straight to my clenching center. The need to submit to his control scares me and turns me on at the same time. I stand tall under the weight of his heated gaze, even as my body liquefies with need. I've been on fire since his serenade on the dance floor. His effect on me is causing a blazing inferno between my thighs.

"Choose your song, Avery," he commands, after a long few second of silence.

That's when I realize I have not moved and have not spoken a word. I remove my iPhone from my purse before tossing it on the desk. I run through my playlist for the perfect song. A song that will fan the flames of this already explosive passion I feel for Lucian. With that in mind, I select the instrumental to *Fever*. It works for what I have in mind for my performance. I want to serenade him just as he did me earlier tonight. I'm not a singer, but I can hold a note, and a spoken word song should be a piece of cake. Right?

The music starts and I snap my fingers in tune with the beat, swaying my hips and gyrating provocatively, as I wrap my arms behind my back. Unzipping my dress, I roll each shoulder, letting the dress slide slowly down my body, teasing Lucian by giving him a peek of my pebbling nipples. When the dress is in a puddle at my feet, channeling Gypsy Rose Lee, I kick it to him.

Lucian's nostrils flare, catching the dress and rubbing it against his cheek. Inhibition gives way to feminine pride. And I continue with the song and dance, walking slowly toward him, exaggerating the sway of my hips and the roll of my shoulders.

For my rendition, I personalize it, substituting Romeo and Juliet with Lucian and Avery. I skip the next verse entirely, choosing to dance only. When I finally straddle him for the lap dance, he is rock solid hard and molten lava hot. I can feel the heat obliterating my black lace thong. My hips move of their own volition, seeking friction against his bulging cock. Lucian's breath quickens, unleashing an inhuman growl from his throat. Desperate for release, I chant, what a lovely way to burn, again and again until I detonate in Lucian's arms. He holds me tight as my body trembles against his.

When my breathing returns to normal, Lucian stands, and I wrap my arms and legs around him. He carries me to the bed, laying me down. Stepping away, he begins to undress. It's not a striptease, but it's fucking hot, nonetheless. In my lust-induced state, I realize I'm still wearing my shoes and pearls. When I sit up to remove them, Lucian shakes his head, stopping me. I lay back watching and waiting for him.

Chapter 10
Lucian

THE STRIPTEASE AND lap dance Avery just performed for me was, without a doubt, one of the sexiest fucking things I've ever seen. I intend to reward her for that. I didn't expect her to serenade me but fuck if that wasn't hot too. The words she chanted as she fell apart in my arms are still dancing around in my head. But words are no longer adequate to express how she makes me feel. It's time I show her.

Climbing into bed with Avery, I spread her legs wide and kneel between her thighs. I take my time removing her shoes. She moans softly when I glide my tongue over her ankles. Leaning forward, I press my lips to her inner thighs. I inhale deeply, taking in her scent, salivating with a desperate need to taste her. Tracing my tongue along the edge of her thong, I tease her with a preview of what's to come. Removing her thong, I toss it aside, before burying my face in her sweet cunt. I claim her with my mouth, plunging my tongue deep inside her. Clasping my hair, Avery holds me in place, fucking my mouth. Her body starts to shake with her impending orgasm.

"Come for me, Rose Petal," I command.

I give her clit a long hard suck and she erupts like Mount St. Helens, quaking uncontrollably.

"Lucian!" she screams, arching her back, begging for more.

I lift her head gently, unraveling the pearls around her neck, letting them fall between her breasts. They are long enough to rest between her thighs. She moans with a sudden intake of breath when I lay them against her folds. With every breath she takes and every move she makes the beads brush against her swollen clit.

My fingers glide gently down the length of her neck to the swells of her breast. I watch her body writhe with tormented pleasure as I travel down her body. Gathering the strands between two fingers, I slowly slide the pearls into her tight wet pussy. Burying my fingers deep inside her, I stretch her wider. She rocks against my hand and her greedy little cunt tightens around my fingers.

"Please," she begs. "I need... Please."

"What do you need?"

"You. More. Always," she recites.

I pull my fingers halfway out, only to push them in again. Thrusting deeper again and again, hitting the cluster of nerves that's sure to drive her crazy. My thumb strokes her clit, rubbing a pearl against the swollen flesh. When her thighs start to tremble, I stop, letting the pressure ease.

"Don't stop," she pants

"Never," I assure her.

I start again in earnest, making her desperate for relief. It only takes a few seconds to have her on edge again. This time when she reaches her peak, I let her shatter.

Removing my fingers, I rope the pearls around my cock. I enter her slowly, allowing her to adjust to the stretching. Filling her completely, I start moving, slow and gentle at first. But when she sticks her tongue in my ear and whispers, "harder," I nearly blow my load. I'll always give Avery what she craves. Thrusting harder and faster, the pearls stroke my cock, overwhelming my senses. And each time Avery clenches around me the feeling is out of this fucking world. If I die today knowing that this was the last time I fucked her, I'll die a happy man.

Sweat drips from my forehead, landing in the hollow of her throat. I fucking love that she is covered in my fluids. I lower my head to kiss her. Moaning into my mouth, Avery deepens the kiss. And when she tears her mouth away, she is breathless and absolutely beautiful with kiss swollen lips.

It feels like every ounce of blood has flowed to my cock. It lengthens and swells as I chase my release. But I can't let go yet. I need Avery with me.

"I need you to come," I growl in her ear. "Come now my rose petal."

On my command she let's go, screaming, "I love you." I follow her seconds later, jerking fiercely, filling her with my seed. Spurt after spurt after spurt until I deflate against her.

I stay planted in her until my cock softens. She whimpers when I pull out, leaving the pearls inside her. I watch her sweet pussy clench and unclench when I yank the pearls out. A tiny aftershock causes her body to tremor. The pearls lay on her stomach coated with our fluids. The vision is erotic for sure. But what has me entranced is the sight of my seed flowing from her and trailing down to her ass crack.

Fuck, I want to claim that too.

After I have come down from my orgasmic high, I check on my girl.

"How do you feel, Avery?"

She responds with grunts and moans. I chuckle, but I need to know if she's okay.

"I need to hear the words, Avery," I urge. "Are you with me?"

She rolls onto her side facing me. Her radiant face glows with a smile.

"Yes, I'm with you and I feel amazing." She leans in to give me a kiss. "I love you, Lucian. I'll always be with you."

My heart swells and so does my cock.

"I love you too," I tell her, caressing her cheek.

We shower and make love once more, before climbing back into bed. Avery falls asleep in my arms, her head resting on my chest, her hand over my heart. It belongs to her now and I know she'll protect it.

• • • •

AVERY AND I HAVE SATURDAY morning to ourselves, however, by lunchtime my family's plans divide us. The women are filling the afternoon with spa treatments and shopping.

The men decide that golfing is a better use of their time. We have lunch at the clubhouse before heading out to the course. I'm distracted, making the afternoon seem endless, since my head is not in the game. My mind goes back to Avery and what awaits us when we return to the city tomorrow. We call it quits after a couple hours, when the sun has gotten the better of us.

Returning to the beach house minutes before Avery, she finds me on the dock. She wraps her arms around my waist from behind me. Resting her cheek on my back, she lets out a soft moan.

"How was the spa and shopping?" I ask

"Relaxing and fun," She giggles. "I have something for you, but it's a surprise."

My mind immediately recalls the first time she had a surprise for me. The precious gift of her submitting to a spanking. My hand and cock twitches, remembering how warm her ass was against my palm. I wanted to make the experience as sensual as possible for her. I wanted her to find pleasure in the pain. To trust me to guide her. To know when she had reached her limit.

"Okay," I say, trying not to sound too eager. But desperately wanting to know what she would be gifting me with this time.

"And how was golfing?"

"Too long," I say instead of upsetting her with my concerns. "And I have a surprise for you too." Surprises are more accurate, I thought, turning to face her.

She beams with delight.

"But you're going to have to wait until tonight."

Pushing up on her tiptoes, she says, "So are you," followed by a quick kiss.

Avery looks exquisite in her platinum floor-length gown. One of the surprises I have in store for her tonight. The satin gown clings to her, accentuating the curves of her body. The split up the right side reveals just enough of her beautifully toned leg. She's wearing her hair down, letting wavy honey brown tresses fall to her shoulders. The make-up she wears only highlights her natural beauty.

As for me, like most men who attend formal events, I'm wearing a tuxedo. It's either designer and custom or not. I'm the former.

When she starts to add the jewelry, she intends to wear, I stop her.

"I have something I want you to wear instead."

Avery meets my gaze in the mirror when I come to stand next to her.

"Another present?" she questions.

"Presents," I clarify.

"You're going to spoil me."

"It's an honor to do so." I admit, before giving her the iconic blue box, the color I'm sure she recognizes.

She hesitates for a moment.

"Take it." I urge.

Avery takes the box, opening it slowly, as if what's inside is going to bite. She gasps when she sees the three-piece collection of platinum and diamonds. The necklace, a choker, consists of three lines of diamonds along the length of the necklace. It matches the single line bracelet perfectly. And diamond stud earrings.

"Lucian, this is too much."

I ignore her comment. "Do you like them?"

"They're exquisite," she says, tracing her finger along the line of the bracelet.

"They're nothing compared to you." She meets my gaze in the mirror again. "Do you like them?" I repeat.

"Yes. It's just..."

I shake my head, silencing her.

"Then they're yours," I say, removing the bracelet from the box. "Give me your wrist."

"She hesitates for a nanosecond, then extends her right arm."

I clasp the bracelet around her wrist, then give her palm a gentle kiss before removing the necklace from the box.

"Hold your hair up for me."

Once the necklace is in place, we stare at our mirror images. Avery's fingertips glide over the lines of the necklace.

"Are you collaring me?"

Her question catches me off guard. I hadn't considered the significance of wearing the choker or what it might mean to her. If I'm honest with myself the idea isn't totally without merit.

"I hadn't thought of it as a collar. That's not why I bought it for you."

"And now?" she queries.

I hold her gaze, letting her see the truth of my desire. "It turns me on, seeing you wear something tangible that says you're mine."

"Will you expect me to wear it every day?"

"Rose Petal, we don't have the typical Dominant/submissive relationship." She nods, and I continue. "We do what feels right for us. I don't need you to wear a collar. You're mine, just as I'm yours.

"I don't think I could wear it publicly every day," she whispers. "But I'll wear it for you on special occasions and in private whenever you want."

"Special occasions and showers," I tease. "I can live with that."

She laughs, and the tension leaves her body, as she pushes each diamond stud through her pierced earlobes. When she's done, she examines her reflection. Her eyes are shining brighter than the diamonds. I offer her my arm and we make our way outside to the limo.

Franklin will be driving us tonight, forgoing the convertible. I want every opportunity to hold my girl in my arms. Once we're settled in the back of the limo, we take the drive to my parent's home.

My parents moved to East Hampton full time the summer before my senior year of high school. It was a transition for me, being away from my friends and the city. The only consolation was that I had Marcus with me for a short time. He was grieving the loss of his parents and the change of scenery had been good for him. After he went back to the city, I made a few new friends, but none that lasted as long as Marcus and Jacob.

• • • •

THE DRIVEWAY OF MY parent's home resembles an automobile showroom, decked with a line of luxury cars on display. The limo falls in line behind the Bentley I recognize as my cousin Julian's who was conspicuously absent from golfing earlier today.

"My father's outdone himself," I say, taking in the view of the enchanting wonderland he has created for my mom.

"It looks like something out of a fairytale," Avery says, peering out the window.

"Ready," I ask.

"I am."

"If I haven't told you already, you're stunningly beautiful tonight." I kiss her tenderly before we exit the limo.

Soft white paper lanterns hang, providing warm and intimate lighting. There's also a purple carpet running along the perfectly manicured lawn, leading to the celebration area. Avery takes my hand, and we follow the path, joining a swarm of East Hampton's finest, dressed to impress.

"Lucian!" someone in the crowd calls out.

Turning in the direction of the voice, I come face-to-face with Gisette Girard, the woman I gave my virginity to. She's nearly twenty years older and I haven't seen her just as long, but she looks great. Avery sees her too, if the grip on my hand is an indication. Gisette maneuvers past the servers carrying appetizers and champagne. Standing directly in front of me, she rests her hand on my left arm. Leaning in, she greets me with air kisses, near each cheek.

"It's so good to see you again, Lucian," she says in French, her native tongue.

"Good to see you too," I respond in English, encouraging her to do the same.

"It's been such a long time, mon cheri." Again, with the French.

"This is my girlfriend, Avery West." I make the introduction, choosing not to respond to her comment. "Avery, this is Gisette Girard."

The women face each other for long seconds before Gisette extends her hand.

"It's actually Gisette Girard-Peters now," she corrects in English.

Avery accepts her hand and says, "Mrs. Peters" by way of greeting.

Releasing Avery's hand, Gisette turns her attention back to me.

"How long are you visiting?" She ignores my frown, continuing in French. "We should meet for lunch to reminisce about old times."

I don't miss her innuendo and neither does Avery. I've had enough of her blatant disrespect.

"There's nothing I care to look back on, my future is beside me."

"I should go find my husband," she says. Finally, getting the message. "He owes me a dance."

Gisette turns to walk away but Avery stops her. "Pardon, Mrs. Peters."

"Yes," Gisette replies.

"Before you choose to have a private conversation, be sure that the conversation is indeed private." Avery delivers her message in perfect French.

Gisette's face is bright red with embarrassment. She turns away and leaves in a huff. Avery knows about my summer fling with Gisette of course. What bothers her is the age difference. I was only fourteen when I gave my virginity to Gisette who was twenty-three at the time. I can't say she doesn't have reasons to resent Gisette. The way she lost her virginity was immeasurably different. But Avery still views it as a violation of a minor. She's not jealous, she just loathes sexual predators.

"How many cougars from your past are ready to pounce?" Avery asks, taking two glasses of champagne from the passing server.

"At this party, I'm not sure," I joke, attempting to lighten the mood.

"Not funny, Thorne."

Accepting the glass of champagne, I take a sip. "Forgive me," I plea.

"For what?"

Before I have a chance to respond my parents approach us. My father is dapper and distinguished in his tuxedo. And my mother is regal in a deep purple floor-length gown. I've never seen her look more radiant.

"Hello, sweethearts." My mom greets us with a hug, sandwiching herself between Avery and me.

After we exchange greetings, my mom steps aside to allow my father to greet us. He's more conservative. A handshake for me and a kiss to the back of the hand for Avery.

Avery and I walk hand-in-hand behind my parents, who are also holding hands. They lead us to a massive tent. The décor is familiar; it reminds me of the restaurant we dined in last night. The tables and chairs are covered in the same white linen, and the chandelier is remarkably similar. There are twenty tables, whereas there were only two last night. Crystal glasses, white fine China, linen napkins, and silver flatware at each place setting atop the table. The centerpiece is different. Although candelabras remain, the bouquets now consist of white roses and a variety of purple flowers.

"How did your parents meet?" Avery asks once we're seated.

Over the years, I've only heard parts of the story. My mom choosing not to discuss how she initially met Charles Thorne, the man who would become my father. But when she had a breakdown, after discovering that my biological father was Avery's adoptive father, she told me everything.

"She was a twenty-year-old nursing student, the night Philip had beaten her and landed her in the hospital." Avery already knows the details of the beating, so I won't rehash that memory. "I told you she had a concussion, however because of it she needed a consultation with neurology."

"Charles?"

"Yes. My dad is a neurosurgeon. He treated her, and she was released from the hospital."

"Did they see each other after she left the hospital?"

"No, according to my dad they were both too broken and it wouldn't have worked. He was recently widowed, and my mom had her own cross to bear."

"What changed, since they're obviously together now?"

"A little over a year later, my dad took Daniel to his pediatrician. My mom was a pediatric nurse. Daniel was playing in the waiting area, and he fell, hitting his elbow. He cried and nothing my dad did soothed him, so my mom went up to them and asked if she could hold Daniel. She took him into her arms, kissed his forehead, and then his elbow. She wiped his tears away and told him he was going to be okay. My dad said she was the first person to ever do that for Daniel."

"Kiss his boo-boo." Avery adds

"Yes. He said he fell for her instantly and he hasn't been able to take his eyes off her since."

"And the rest is history." Avery echoes my thought.

I lift the dinner menu, giving it a quick read.

"What looks good?" Avery asks, peeking at my menu.

There is a dinner menu at each place setting, emblazoned with ornate calligraphy. The dinner options listed are mouthwatering.

"The salmon looks good." I don't care for quail, and I had the filet mignon last night.

Avery nods in agreement, taking a sip of her champagne, finishing the glass. She appears nervous for some unknown reason.

"Did you get your parents an anniversary gift?"

"They didn't want me to buy them anything, so instead I donated one hundred thousand dollars in their names to their favorite charity."

"That's very generous of you."

"It's a worthy cause." One I support one hundred percent. I don't say the last part.

"I didn't get them anything," she says, lowering her head.

"Is that what's making you anxious?" I take her hand in mine. "They ask everyone not to bring a gift. They just want everyone to share in their celebration."

"Okay," she says. "I'll have the salmon too." Her uncertain tone and the change of subject gives me pause. But I don't question her about it.

Avery and I choose the Horseradish Crusted Salmon Medallion with Dilled Cucumbers and Mustard Sauce. There are two other choices: The Seared Filet of Beef with Potato Gnocchi, and Swiss Chard, and the Roasted Quail Stuffed with Mushrooms, Quinoa, and Foie Gras. There's also an option for vegetarians.

Shortly after dinner Avery excuses herself from the table. I watch her walk up to the band leader. After they have exchanged a few words, the violinist passes Avery the instrument.

"What's she doing?" my mom asks. She's obviously as curious as I am.

"I'm not sure yet," I reply, without taking my eyes off Avery.

The singer gives Avery the microphone. Clutching it tightly, I can see the nervousness riding her slumped shoulders.

"Excuse me," Avery says, gaining everyone's attention. "I haven't known Charles and Lucinda long, so I wasn't sure what gift I could give them for their anniversary. What I do know for certain is that they only have eyes for each other. This is my gift to them. Happy anniversary." She concludes, securing the microphone on the pole.

The guitars start to strum, followed by the bass player. Avery lifts the violin, anchoring it with her shoulder and chin. Closing her eyes, she begins to play. Her fingers move with precision as she glides the bow effortlessly over the strings. The threat of tears temporarily clouds my vision of her. My heart fills with joy. And I am so proud that she has chosen to share her gift with my parents. She never ceases to amaze me.

The entire room is held captive by her performance, but I'm enslaved by the woman. When the ballad comes to an end, everyone is on their feet applauding. I'm on my feet before she returns the violin. As Avery makes her way back to our table, amongst the guests stopping her to show appreciation, I realize all the attention may be daunting for her. She doesn't like being in a crowd or having strangers invade her personal space.

Reaching her, I take her hand, pulling her against my body. I kiss her, blocking out the voices for both of us. I break the kiss and tell her how wonderful she is.

"The guests of honor would like to thank you," I say before whisking her away from the crowd.

When Avery and I return to our table, everyone is standing to greet us. To greet her. My mom pulls Avery into a tight hug, holding her for long seconds.

"Thank you, sweetheart." My mother's throat clogs with unshed tears.

Releasing Avery, my mom steps aside to allow my father to thank her. He does so with a kiss to each cheek.

"You play beautifully, my dear," he says. "But how did you know, I Only Have Eyes for You, is our song?"

"It was the only song you danced to at Daniel's fundraiser." Avery clears her throat and continues. "And you referenced it in your toast last night. I just assume it was for sentimental reasons."

"You're very observant," my father compliments.

"It's my writer's eye," she says, lowering her gaze slightly.

While the statement is true, it's far more than that. Being aware of her surroundings has become second nature to her. If she were not a writer, she'd make an excellent detective. My father smiles and nods because he knows there's more as well.

Raina, Evelyn, and Conrad are next, enveloping her into a family hug. Everyone else compliments her on how well she played and slowly the dinner conversation topic changes. Avery visibly relaxes when she's no longer the center of attention.

"How did it feel to play again?" I ask when I have her in my arms on the dance floor.

"It felt okay," she hedges

"Just okay." I want her to share this with me. I could tell it's important to her. She was practically glowing as she played the violin.

"I didn't know I missed it so much. The weight of the violin on my shoulder. My fingers against the strings and the glide of the bow." She takes a deep breath. "It felt really good. It felt like I was a part of the music. I remembered playing for my mom and I wanted to play for her again."

"I'm sure the angels heard you playing today." She leans into me, resting her head on my chest.

"Thank you," she whispers

"Why are you thanking me?"

"For loving me and for knowing what to say to make me feel better."

"Always," I say, kissing the top of her head.

• • • •

WE ARRIVE HOME WELL after midnight. The moon and the stars shining in the night sky pales in comparison to the beautiful woman beside me. Anticipating the surprise Avery promised me, has me wide awake. I feel like a kid waiting up for Santa. Like the night before, I scoop her up in my arms and carry her to our bedroom.

"Unzip me please," she says, standing with her back to me.

I slide the zipper down her dress, revealing the delicate line of her spine. Unable to resist, I bend down to place a kiss at the small of her back, just above the line of her red thong. My favorite color.

"I'll be right back," she says, walking away.

Disappearing into the walk-in closet for a moment, she returns without her dress. Standing before me is a goddess wearing a short white satin nightgown and the sexiest red bottom high heels I've ever seen. Enthralled by her beauty, it takes me a moment to notice she's carrying a gift bag.

"This is for you," she says, giving me the bag, before taking a seat in the chair I sat in last night for my lap dance. She looks majestic sitting there with her legs crossed, waiting for me to open the gift. "It's more like an us gift."

Opening the bag, I pull out the contents. I stare at the box I now hold in my hands and only three words come to mind. Lucky. Fucking. Bastard.

The box contains an assortment of butt plugs. A total of four, in varying sizes. There's also lube inside the box. She has thought of everything.

"I read that anal is best when you prep for it. I thought we could start with the smallest and work our way up to your cock."

The confidence in her voice hardens my dick more than the thought of claiming her ass. But another thought deflates my hard-on.

"You got this while you were out shopping with my mom and Evelyn?"

"No silly," she smirks. "I went on my own while they were getting massages."

I have no doubt that women share a lot about their sex life with each other. Especially best friends. However, I have no desire to share my sexual proclivities with anyone but Avery. Least of all my mother and sister.

Avery uncross her legs, giving me an unfettered view, and my basic instinct is to drop to my knees and bury my face between her thighs. There's something about her sitting there in a white satin nightgown, wearing sky high heels and having the confidence to initiate anal sex. The virginal white says innocence, while the heels, butt plugs, and my collar screams debauchery. The contradiction is absofuckinglutely sexy.

"We start tonight."

"Yes, Sir."

She's fucking perfect and mine.

I want her relaxed before we begin anal play. An orgasm or two will ensure that. Desperate for a taste, I drop to my knees before her. Spreading her wide, I bury my face in her sweet cunt. Devouring her. Savoring her. Loving her.

It takes me no time to get her off. Pleasuring her with my mouth and fingers, telling her all the bad things I want to do with her.

I stand and pull her up on her feet with me. Kissing her tenderly, she moans when she tastes her essence on my tongue.

Breaking the kiss, I tell her to raise her arms above her head. She does as I ask. I lift the hem of her nightgown, pulling it up slowly, my fingers and the satin material glides over her soft skin. Inch by inch, I expose her flat belly, her full luscious breasts, and her shoulders, until the nightgown is over her head and puddling at her feet.

"I want you on the bed, on your hands and knees."

Avery follows my command without hesitation, climbing onto the bed and getting into position. Her curvy ass pointing directly at me, I grab the lube and the smallest plug and climb onto bed behind her. I want to possess her in every way, every inch of her. But I don't want to push her beyond what she can handle. Pressing my lips to her spine, I trail kisses down to her ass cheeks. She gasps and moans.

"Are you sure?" I ask, before we continue, but silently praying she hasn't changed her mind.

"I trust you, Lucian. I'm sure."

"What's your safe word, Avery?" I always ask for her benefit not mine.

"Lighthouse," she whispers

"Use it if you need to. But all you need to say is stop and I will. You mean too much to me to ever hurt you."

"I know," she says. "I love you too."

"We're going to start with my finger."

She nods, and I proceed, coating my finger with the lube and squirting some between her ass cheeks. Inserting my finger slowly and gently, I feel the resistance immediately. I push deeper, breeching the muscle.

"Lucian!" she cries out.

I stop, holding still inside her, allowing her body to accept the invasion.

"I'm here, Rose Petal."

I reach around between her thighs, rubbing her clit. The simultaneous stimulation has her coming for the second time in under a minute. My finger sinks deeper into her tight ass, stroking her gently and stretching her. When she starts pushing back against my hand, I pull out, replacing my finger with the smallest plug.

"Fuck," she groans

I work the plug, thrusting it in and out of Avery's ass. Pushing against my hand, Avery clenches and unclenches her muscles around the plug.

"You're so beautiful, and you're mine."

"More... Please Lucian. More."

I want her begging for me to fill her ass with my cock. Pulling out, I switch to a larger plug. She offers very little resistance. When I reach for her clit this time she's soaked.

"You're so fucking wet," I growl. My dick is so goddam hard it can drill a hole through granite. "I'm going to fill your ass with this plug while I fuck your sweet pussy. You're going to love it. I promise."

I move away from her, and she moans. Climbing out of bed, I leave the plug buried in her ass. With a butt plug up her ass, Avery is all my fantasies made real. She is everything I never knew I needed.

"Lay on your back for me." Again, she complies. "Spread your legs for me and stroke your clit." She moans softly when her finger brushes against her swollen flesh. "I want to see you pleasure yourself."

I watch her stroke and tease herself, writhing against her own hand. She watches as I undress, working her fingers faster with each item of clothing I remove. She brings herself to an orgasm just as my boxer briefs drop to my ankles.

Climbing back into bed, I lay between her thighs. Sliding into her inch by inch, I urge her to take all of me. The presence of the plug makes her pussy tighter. She feels so good, so fucking wet and tight. I thrust into her, driving deeper, hitting her G-spot over and over. She digs her nails into my back screaming my name. Her moans and cries of pleasure has me losing control. The need to possess her completely fuels my passion. I pound into her harder, again and again. Consumed by an undeniable craving, I don't let up. The headboard slams against the wall fiercely as I fuck her. She has given me the right to take her exactly how I want. She gave it to me with her trust. A trust I will never break or dishonor. When her safe word doesn't come, I know we have transcended it.

"Come for me." The words are a growl deep in my throat.

Avery trembles beneath me, her greedy little cunt holding my cock tight.

"Lucian!" she screams. "I'm coming."

I thrust harder and faster chasing my release until we fall over the edge together, crashing in a powerful explosion. Breathless, I cling to her, never wanting to let her go.

We lay together bonded by sweat, semen, and lube. And all I can think is, I fucking love this woman. When I pull out of her, she whimpers and reach for me.

"Shower with me, Rose Petal," I say, climbing out of bed.

I follow her to the bathroom and the sight of the butt plug still in her curvy ass has my dick twitching for more.

• • • •

ON OUR LAST DAY IN the Hamptons, Avery and I meet my family at 10 a.m. for Sunday brunch at my parent's house. It's a smaller gathering compared to the last two days. My parents, Avery and I, as well as Katelyn and Daniel. We're all gathered at the table when Daniel stands and says he has an announcement. At the back of my mind I already know what he's going to say.

"I'm in love with Chris." Clearing his throat, he clarifies. "Christopher Adams."

The room falls silent for a moment. Our mother is the first to speak.

"I know," she says. "Why isn't he here?"

A look of astonishment and relief contorts Daniel's features.

"I wanted to do this alone. He's back at the hotel."

"Have him come join us," our father commands

Daniel nods, pulling out his cell he sends a text. The incoming reply is almost immediate.

"He'll be here soon," Daniel relays.

Taking his seat, Daniel tries to relax, but I can see he's still anxious.

"Are you going public with this, during your campaign?" Katelyn asks.

"I'm not sure yet. My first step was to come out to my family."

"What does Chris think?" she asks

"He says it's my choice, but I should be honest with the voters."

"I agree, you're running a good clean campaign. You have nothing to be ashamed of," our father chimes in.

"I'm not ashamed," Daniel defends. "I want to win, and this may negatively impact my political aspirations."

"It could either way," Katelyn says.

"Any advice, Lucian?" Daniel asks. "You seem to have mastered the court of public opinion."

"The truth doesn't change, Daniel. Whether it's now or later. Right now, you can control the narrative. Waiting and hoping no one outs you during your campaign is risky."

"I guess I have a lot to think about. Thanks," he says.

The housekeeper escorts Chris to the dining room about twenty minutes later. He greets everyone before taking a seat next to Daniel. My mom immediately starts questioning him, wanting to know more about him and his family. It's her way of welcoming him. Chris smiles, graciously, answering her questions. The conversation turns to the next time we can all be together again. Avery wants us to host another dinner party, so we all agree to meet a month from now, after my parents are back from their trip abroad.

A few hours later, Avery and I are on the road back to Manhattan.

Chapter 11

Avery

WHEN I WAKE ON MONDAY morning, Lucian has already gone. The past three days, while extremely enjoyable, came at a price. Lucian rearranging his schedule meant there were things he needed to take care of on his first day back at the office. One of the many things the time away gave me was a renewed love of the violin. My mission today is to retrieve and repair my old violin. It may be too small for me now, but I want to keep it for sentimental reasons. My plan is to purchase something new. I'm ready to play again; ready to fill my heart and home with music again.

With an itinerary in mind, I text William, my driver and bodyguard. Giving myself only an hour to be ready, I spring out of bed, sprinting to the shower. I'm in and out in under five minutes. Smiling inwardly, I recall the shower two nights ago. My center clenches, reacting to how full I felt with a butt plug in my ass and Lucian's cock filling my pussy. The shower was one of the longest we've ever had together. When he finally removed the plug, I mourned the loss of it and suddenly felt empty. We haven't used the two larger plugs yet. I'm eagerly waiting to try them out. Lucian was as gentle and patient as I knew he would be. Afterwards, he took care of me, holding me in his arms, whispering how much he loves me until the last words I hear are, "I'm going to marry you, Avery West." I know it wasn't a proposal, but when the time comes there can be only one answer. Yes.

Now that I've showered and dressed, I need food. Maggie is in the kitchen when I get there.

"Good morning, Miss West," she says. "What would you like for breakfast?"

I'm trying to accept someone other than myself taking care of my needs. Being Lucian Thorne's live-in girlfriend comes with certain perks I'm not sure I will ever be comfortable with. I tell myself it's a fair trade off. Three days out of the week Lucian and I can be a normal couple. I make dinner for him or we're in the kitchen preparing a meal together. But what's normal when your boyfriend's a billionaire and can have anything he wants? A timer goes off, and Maggie is still waiting for my answer.

"Good morning, Maggie," I reply, "just, coffee and an omelet."

"Your usual?" she asks

"Yes, thanks."

Humming a song, I don't recognize, Maggie pours me a cup of coffee. Then goes about making the omelet. When she's done, she plates the omelet, placing it in front of me. I thank her again, before taking the first bite.

Finishing my breakfast, I swallow the last sip of my coffee. Now that I'm nourished, I'm ready to head out on my mission. Padding barefoot down the hall to the bedroom, I slip on my sandals and grab my purse.

William is in the foyer waiting for me when I return. "Are you ready to go, Miss West?" he asks.

"All set," I say, heading to the elevator.

William follows me. We take the elevator down to the parking garage. Since I have already given him my itinerary, we ride in silence, which is usually the case.

Arriving at my apartment building in Chelsea, we take the stairs down to the basement. Where I have a storage unit. I have rented my apartment furnished, but the personal items I didn't take with me when I moved in with Lucian are stored here. I rummage through the box labelled music until I find what I'm looking for. My old violin packed away in its case.

Opening the case, I view the damage I did to the instrument so long ago. The bow is broken in half, the strings are no longer attached to the violin, and two of the tuning pegs are missing.

I took the anger I felt out on the last gift my mom ever gave me. I remember the incident clearly, as if it were yesterday. I told the guidance counselor at my school about the neglect and abuse. I could tell by the horrified look on her face that she believed me. Child Protective Services visited my home that same evening. Yet, regardless of my allegations, they believed Philip when he told them I was grieving and lashing out. After they had gone, Philip had a drink and left the apartment without saying a word to me. In a fit of anger, I blamed my mother for dying and leaving me alone. That's when I picked up the violin and began taking my rage out on it. When I had calmed down again, I packed it away neatly and I haven't seen it until this moment.

Buried in the past, I didn't hear William come up behind me.

"Are you okay, Miss West?" he asks

Looking up at him, I can't see his face through my blurry vision.

And I realize I'd been crying loud enough for him to be concerned.

I nod, trying to regain my composure.

"Should I call Mr. Thorne?" The worry in his voice is evident.

"No, I'm fine." I say.

Closing the violin case, I carry it out of the storage room. We're on our way to Sam Ash Music store when I decide to call Lucian. He answers on the first ring.

"Hello beautiful," he sighs.

The sound of his voice makes me feel better almost immediately.

"I hope I'm not disturbing you. But I didn't get a chance to say good morning."

"Good morning, beautiful." He chuckles, and the sound caresses me all over. "What are the odds that I need to hear your voice at the exact time you're calling?"

I needed to hear his voice too. To wrap myself in his deep soothing tone.

"I'd say the odds are forever in your favor, Mr. Thorne. I'll always be here when you need me."

"The same goes for me. Always."

"I love you."

"I love you too," he says, and my world is set right again.

We end the call and I know we are made better by the few minutes we spoke.

William pulls up to the curb outside Sam Ash Music on West 34th Street. Sam Ash Music has been serving musicians since 1924. They have a large selection at a great price. The shop has moved since the last time I visited with my mom. But the atmosphere is just as I remember it.

A musician sales associate greets me when I walk in. A man in his mid-thirties.

"Good morning, how can I help you?" He smiles warmly.

Placing the violin case on a nearby counter, I say hello.

"Can you fix this?" I ask, opening the case.

He leans in to inspect the damage. Removing the instrument from the case, he gives it a thorough examination.

"Our repair shop can handle all string instrument repairs, including installing new strings, repairing the tailpiece, and the tuning pegs. If you leave it with us, we'll call you with an estimate."

He completes a repair form, taking my name and phone number, and he promises to have an estimate within the hour.

"Thank you," I say when he gives me my copy of the repair order form.

I look around the shop at the instruments. When I spot the selection of violins, I'm overcome with joy. Surely there's something here for me. I do find a few that I like, but the F.R. Pfretszchner Model 150 is made of beautifully hand-carved European Spruce on the top and hand-carved European solid flamed Maple on the back, sides, neck, and scroll. The expert craftmanship makes this violin the only choice for me.

The violin is already strung. Lifting it to my shoulder, I test the reach by playing a note with my pinky finger. It's the right size. Testing the bow against the strings, I begin to play a few notes. There are only two other customers in the store, and no one seems to mind. I check the price on the violin and decide it's worth the cost. I'm in search of sheet music when the musician sales associate offers some assistance. I follow him to the section for classical jazz and R&B. I find what I'm looking for and now I'm ready to check out.

Holding my purchases like found treasure, I make my way to the car, with William trailing behind me. The smile on my face replaces the sadness I felt earlier. I can't wait to share my treasure with Lucian.

Chapter 12
Lucian

MONDAY MORNING I'M back at the office bright and early. I'm wrapping up a video conference call when the phone on my desk rings.

"Mr. Thorne, detectives Turner and Dodd are here to see you," Helen, my assistant informs me.

Dodd. Why does that name sound familiar?

"Give me five minutes, then send them in," I instruct.

"Yes, sir," she says before ending the call.

The detectives enter my office a few minutes later. The first, an older man in his mid-fifties, takes in his surroundings before speaking.

"Nice view," he compliments. "I'm Detective George Turner of the NYPD and this is my partner Detective Joseph Dodd."

The other detective is younger, maybe a few years older than me. His eyes are trained on me, as if he has weighed and measured me and found me lacking.

"Mr. Thorne and I have met before," Dodd says. "Ten years ago."

The memory of a young police officer questioning Franklin and I become clear. The night we found Avery abused and in shock, after she had gotten away from the man who raped and held her captive for weeks.

"Yes," I say, taking measure of him as a man as well. "I remember you, Officer Dodd."

He frowns, clearly irritated by the incorrect use of his title.

"That's Homicide Detective Dodd," he asserts.

"What can I do for you?" I ask, offering them a seat.

The detectives take the two seats directly in front of my desk. Taking my seat, I wait for an answer.

"We recently received new evidence involving the deaths of your wife and son. We would like to ask you a few questions and give you a chance to amend your statement." Dodd's assertion is loaded with accusation.

I clutch the arm of my chair, holding back the rage heating my blood.

"In a heighten situation the memory can be faulty." Turner adds.

"I don't need to amend my statement. The truth doesn't change. Ever."

I reach into my desk drawer and pull out two business cards. I slide the cards across the desk to Turner and Dodd.

"What's this?" Turner asks, picking up the card.

Standing, I say, "My attorney."

"It would be in your best interests to cooperate, Thorne." Dodd stands, eyeing me with undisguised animosity.

"I intend to after you contact my attorney and make an appointment." I hit the button to open my office door. "Until then we're done. You can see yourselves out."

Dodd smirks, leaving the business card on my desk before walking out. Turner follows.

I close the door to my office, shutting out the world.

"My iPhone rings and the name on the display immediately changes my mood."

"Hello, beautiful," I say, wishing I was home when she woke up.

"I hope I'm not disturbing you. But I didn't get a chance to say good morning." Her voice is playful, but I hear the need in it.

"Good morning, beautiful," I chuckle, my own voice strained. "What are the odds that I need to hear your voice at the exact time you're calling?"

She may have called because she needs me, but I need her just as much.

"I'd say the odds are forever in your favor, Mr. Thorne. I'll always be here when you need me."

My heart melts.

"The same goes for me. Always."

"I love you," she says, and my world is set right again.

"I love you too."

With my world back on its axis, spinning correctly again, I give Jake a call, to relay the details of the meeting with the NYPD detectives Turner and Dodd.

"You should expect a call from them," I tell him.

"I'll get a copy of the accident report and review all the statements before we meet with the detectives," he assures me.

Before he stepped into the corporate world of mergers and acquisitions, Jacob Gannon was a very successful defense attorney and a shark in the courtroom. He's great at what he does and he's the attorney I call when I need the best.

"Thanks Jake, I'll talk to you soon."

Ending the call, I return to work, powering through my packed schedule, finding solace in the routine until I'm with Avery again.

It's after seven o'clock in the evening when I arrive home. Entering the foyer, I instantly notice two things. The first is the appetizing smell of dinner wafting in the air. And the second is music. It takes me a second or two to recognize the harmonious strings of a violin playing At Last, the song I sang to Avery while we danced. I follow the direction of the music to the bedroom Avery is using as a home office. I observe her from the doorway. Her eyes are closed and as she plays, she hums the lyrics. Watching her, I'm spellbound by the glow on her face and the ease at which she plays. She's amazing. My woman has it all. Brains. Beauty. Talent.

When she finishes the song, her lips curl into a smile. Opening her eyes, she looks up at me. Her gaze holds mine with expectant joy. She lays the violin down on the chair she vacates.

"I wanted to surprise you."

"And you did." I lean in and press my lips to her forehead. "Coming home to you playing our song is just what I needed."

"Our song." She smiles, nodding in agreement.

The song speaks to the heart of our love, the deep yearning for it, the relief at finding it, and the undeniable rapture at claiming it. At Last.

Taking me by the hand, Avery leads me down the hall to the kitchen. She wash her hands before plating our dinner. I remove my suit jacket, wash my hands, and select a bottle of wine. We're seated at the breakfast bar when Avery asks about my day.

"Do you want to talk about what's bothering you?"

She has become adept at reading my moods. In the short time we've been together I can honestly say, she knows me better than anyone. I tell her about the visit to my office from the NYPD detectives Turner and Dodd. And my call to Jake.

"I have no clue what new evidence the police have or why homicide detectives are investigating an accident that happened over three years ago."

"They can't possibly think you had anything to do with the accident."

"At this point they only want to question me." Inhaling deeply, I pause before I tell her the rest. "Samantha has filed a civil suit against me, claiming damages due to the car accident. She's suing me for fifteen million dollars."

"Oh my god," Avery gasps in surprise. "Do you think the civil suit is why the police want to question you?"

"I was served as I was leaving Thorne Tower this evening, so I would bet on it."

"I'm coming with you. When are we going to the police station?"

"Jake has made an appointment for ten tomorrow morning."

Avery is quiet for a moment, and I remember she wasn't quite herself when she called me this morning.

"It's your turn," I challenge. "Why were you upset this morning?"

"What did William tell you?" she accuses. "I told him not to call you. It was a case of reliving a bad memory."

"He didn't say anything."

The look of confusion lifts her brows.

"How did you know I'd been crying?"

"I told you, I'm always aware of you." Stroking her cheek tenderly I tell her, "I heard it in your voice."

Avery fills me in on the details of her morning. How, finding her broken violin neatly packed away triggered memories of how she blamed her mother for dying and leaving her alone. How that led to her destroying the last gift her mother gave her. Avery admits that she's having the violin repaired for sentimental reasons, since it's too small for her to play.

"I didn't realize I'd been crying," she sighs. "It was cathartic. When the tears stopped, I knew I could play for my mom again. I felt ashamed for blaming her for the things that happened to me after she died. So, I packed the shame away with the broken violin."

"I understand. When Camille and Ian died, I went through a period where I blamed myself, but I also blamed Camille. I blamed her for leaving me and killing my son in doing so. It wasn't until recently that I let it go. I forgave her, and I forgave myself. Your mother loved you, Avery, and there's no way anyone who truly loves you will ever willingly leave you."

"Deciding to play the violin for your parents made me understand how much it's a part of me. And by locking that part of me away, I was still in a sense blaming my mom. I knew I had to let go of the shame and forgive myself."

After dinner Avery and I settle in for a quiet night, watching a movie. A little after ten we decide it's time for bed. We make love in the shower, climbing into bed immediately after. Despite the events of the day, sleep comes easily for us, drifting off moments after our heads hit the pillow.

• • • •

JAKE, AVERY AND I ARRIVE at the police station fifteen minutes before the scheduled appointment time. We're only there a few minutes before we are taken to a conference room, or maybe an interrogation room is more accurate. Jake and Avery take seats at the metal table in the center of the room. I remain standing since I'm too wired. I need to move, to burn off the excess energy. I don't know how long I pace the room before the door opens. Turner walks in first, followed by Dodd. They take seats across from Jake and Avery. When Jake signals me to do the same, I take the seat between my council and my girlfriend.

The detectives start by introducing themselves.

"For the record would you all state your names please?" Turner asks.

"I'm Jacob Gannon, Mr. Thorne's attorney," Jake says, giving both detectives a business card.

I introduce myself directly to the camera, which has come on since the detectives entered the room.

Avery introduces herself, by name only, holding my hand under the table.

"Are you Thorne's attorney too, Miss West?" Dodd asks.

"I'm sure you already know the answer to that, Detective Dodd," she answers, "Unless you've been living under a rock these past few weeks?"

I give her hand a gentle squeeze. She's angry for me and she's not in the mood for his pretense. He's aware that she's my girlfriend and I'm sure he knows she is the same girl he questioned me about ten years ago. That night has impacted the three of us. For him to feign ignorance is ridiculous, especially when the tabloids and even legitimate media outlets have made sure that the names Marisa Hunter and Avery West will forever be linked.

"Shall we get down to it then?" Turner interjects.

Jake nods, encouraging Turner to begin his questions.

"Mr. Thorne, in your statement three years ago, you said that your wife was leaving you and taking your son with her. Did you try to stop her physically?" Turner asks.

Jake signals me not to answer; instead, he pulls out a stack of papers from his briefcase.

"Gentlemen, I've taken the liberty of obtaining a copy of Mr. Thorne's original statement." Jake hands out the copies. "If you'd refer to page three, paragraph two, where the highlighted sections begin."

Jake read my statement verbatim. "In response to your question, Detective Turner, Mr. Thorne clearly states that there was no physical altercation with his wife. Therefore, we have no need to offer any further response to your question."

"When you followed her, what were your intentions?" Turner follows up.

Jake points out the next highlighted section. "That question has also been answered."

"Did you know that your wife was having an affair with your brother before the night of the car crash?" Dodd asks.

The statement from three years ago never mentions Camille's affair with Daniel or the fact that she thought Ian was Daniel's son.

"Where are you going with this?" Jake queries.

"Are you going to instruct your client to answer the question, Mr. Gannon?"

"Not until you tell us what this is about," Jake responds

Unfortunately, I already know what this is about. The only way the police would know about Camille's affair is if Samantha told them. She's trying to paint me as the jealous husband, who came after his wife in a fit of anger. This only makes her civil suit stronger, whether there's any evidence of criminal wrongdoing or not.

"Some forms of civil wrongs are also crimes, Mr. Thorne. A civil claim for wrongful death may also result in a criminal charge of homicide." Dodd gives me an arrogant smirk when he adds, "Making this case both a criminal and a civil matter. It's in your best interest to cooperate fully."

"If you had any evidence of a crime, you would be arresting my client, not making thinly veiled threats, Detective Dodd."

"Your client is the only suspect in an ongoing investigation of a possible double vehicular homicide. Believe me when I tell you that making veiled threats are not necessary when evidence against your client is piling up."

"If you don't have any other questions for my client or an arrest warrant, this interrogation is over."

Jake stands when the detective doesn't ask another question or produce an arrest warrant. I stand with Avery's hand still in mine, leading her to the door.

"Take care, Miss West," Dodd taunts as we're leaving.

Red hot rage consumes me, and I turn to face him. How fucking dare this little prick insinuate that I'm a danger to Avery? She must have sensed my anger, as her small hand holds mine tight. And when she turns to face Dodd, she's the picture of serenity.

"Detective Dodd, I think your bias opinions toward Mr. Thorne is clouding your perspective. You seem to have tried and convicted him without any evidence. And here I thought that the judgement is left up to the jury. Maybe I should ask my surrogate father Judge Conrad Preston, or maybe he could ask his good friends the commissioner and the mayor. I'm sure one of them has the answer."

"Is that a threat, Miss West? Do you think that throwing your connections at me will get me to back off?"

"What I think detective is that you should show a little respect for your badge if nothing else." With that Avery turns and walks out of the room.

My gaze follows her, but I don't miss the stunned stares from the other men in the room. Jake's chuckle breaks the silence.

"Don't let her get away." Jake says for my ears only.

Taking his advice, I follow her, knowing I'll never let her go.

Chapter 13
Avery

I WALK OUT OF THE INTERROGATION room feeling pissed. Detective Dodd seems to have a grudge against Lucian. But that's not what is making me furious. It's the civil suit Samantha has filed, which may be the reason for the detective's animosity towards Lucian. He believes that Lucian is responsible for the deaths of his wife and child. I knew the bitch was bat shit crazy and nothing but trouble the moment I laid eyes on her. I also know it's not about the money; she wants Lucian.

It doesn't take long for the footsteps to reach me. Lucian takes my hand, and Jake follows us out of the precinct. Franklin is at the curb waiting for us. He opens the back-passenger door and I climb in. Lucian speaks with Jake briefly, before he climbs in beside me.

"Come here." Lucian reaches for me. "You were like a lioness defending her cub in there, all teeth and claws."

Sitting on Lucian's lap, I snuggle against his chest, relaxing in his strong arms. He has always been my protector, and now it's time I did the same for him.

"I defend what's mine."

I feel Lucian's lips curve into a smile against my hair.

"Jake will meet us at my office to discuss strategy."

"Will he file a motion to dismiss the civil suit?"

"That's not the impression I got. He wants to know what evidence the other side has."

I nod, understanding we need to know what we're up against, in order to form a battle plan. With nothing else to say, we continue the ride to Thorne Tower in silence.

The paparazzi are waiting outside Thorne Tower when the limo pull up to the curb. Franklin opens the back-passenger door and Lucian climbs out. Accepting his offered hand, I follow him. Lucian holds me close as we make our way past the paparazzi. Franklin, who is now joined by William, flanks us. They clear a path for Lucian and me. But that doesn't stop the questions being hurled at us.

"Lucian is it true that the police are investigating you for the vehicular homicide of your wife and child?"

"Avery, will you stand by Lucian if he's convicted?"

"Mr. Thorne!" The voice yells over the crowd. "Did you kill your wife and son in a fit of road rage because she cheated on you with your brother?"

Lucian stops, turning to face the mob of gossip hungry vultures. With military like precision Franklin and William turn with him.

"Find out who said that." Lucian whispers to Franklin, before addressing the crowd

"No comment," he says, blanketing their faces.

"Is that all you have to say for yourself, Mr. Thorne?" There's that voice again.

Lucian and Franklin turn to face the voice in the crowd. Franklin walks toward the man and Lucian turns away without uttering another word. Thorne's security officers greet us at the door and the crowd backs away. We enter Thorne Tower and William returns to the BMW.

This is the first time I've walked through the lobby of Thorne Tower by Lucian's side. The perspective is very different. When Lucian enters the massive kingdom, he has built, his subjects are happy to see him. They all greet him warmly, and he responds in kind. He remembers all their names, engaging in small talk and asking about their families.

When we enter the reception area of Lucian's office, he instructs Helen, his assistant, to inform Jake and Carter to be in his office in thirty minutes.

Behind closed doors, Lucian pulls me into his arms, holding me against his body. Letting out a harsh breath, his self-assured composure abandons him as he struggles to regain control. My arm tightens around his waist, hoping it offers some reassurance. I don't know how long we stand there before Lucian moves us to the couch. I'm sitting on his lap when he whispers, "Thank you."

"Why are you thanking me?"

"For being what I need."

I lift my chin, and Lucian accepts my offer, covering my mouth with his. The kiss is gentle at first, slow and savoring. Then it turns into an all-consuming hunger, devouring my moans of pleasure and filling me with an insatiable need. He nips and sucks my bottom lip ravenously and growls when I reciprocate.

Lucian manages to lay me flat on my back, covering me with his muscular body. His hand slides up my thigh, slipping his finger under the edge of my panties. I moan when his finger presses against my clit, sending sharp volts of electricity through me.

His lips brush against my ear. "I need you," he hisses.

I spread my legs wider in response. Desperate for him, I lift my hips, pleading for release. Lucian seals his mouth over mine, kissing me so deep, the force of it takes my breath away.

We're interrupted when Helen's voice comes through the intercom.

"Mr. Thorne, Mr. Gannon and Mr. Lincoln are here as requested," she says.

We lie there for a moment, and I wish the world would go away. But running away from our problems is not our style.

"Give me five minutes and send them in," Lucian instructs.

Lucian stands, pull me up with him and lead me to his private bathroom. We freshen up, but Lucian is still hard, his erection prominent against his slacks. His gaze follows mine.

"It can't be helped. But once we're done with this meeting, I owe you an orgasm," he vows.

We take seats at the table in his office and wait for Jake and Carter. The door opens and Carter enters first, followed by Jake. They join us at the table. Jake sits on Lucian's left and Carter sits on his right next to me.

Jake speaks first.

"I've filed an answer in response to the claims made against Lucian, and I've requested that the case be moved into the pre-trial phase within a week. Carter says that's enough time for him to gather the evidence we need to get Samantha's claim dropped."

"Why can't we go straight to motion to dismiss?" I ask.

"We want to know what evidence they're planning to present if this thing goes to trial. During the initial stages of the lawsuit each party involved discloses evidence. It's called discovery, the process of exchanging evidence and statements between the parties. It's meant to eliminate surprises, clarify what the lawsuit is about, and give the parties the opportunity to decide if they should settle or drop the claim."

"Do you think this is a valid claim? Is that why you're not filing a motion to dismiss?"

"No, I know it's bullshit," Jake says adamantly. "But the attorney Samantha has retained is very good, almost as good as me. She wouldn't take the case if the evidence didn't support the claim."

"So, how are you going to refute her claims?"

Jake looks at Lucian and back at me. His expression is unreadable, like the man we have both sworn to defend.

"The claims against Lucian are serious, but they're also a lie, which means that Samantha has manufactured whatever evidence she gave her lawyer to convince her to take the case. I can and will disprove it. Can you trust me to do that?"

I nod, and Lucian takes my hand in his.

"Carter is handling the investigation." Lucian assures me. "We'll get what we need to end this."

I can't help but worry. If Samantha is manufacturing evidence, she has gone off the deep end. She must know that Lucian has the resources to invalidate her claims. This isn't her end game; she has something bigger planned.

"She was waiting for you to choose her," I say interrupting the exchange between the men. "But you never did, so now she wants to punish you and she doesn't care how the punishment comes about. She's delusional and she could be dangerous."

"She's under 24-hour surveillance, so she won't get near you," Carter says.

"I'm not worried about me. Her delusions are fixated on Lucian. What if she believes that he has betrayed her somehow by not choosing her?"

My eyes cloud with tears, the thought of losing Lucian is too unbearable to fathom. A single tear trail down my cheek and Lucian wipes it away.

"Excuse me," I say leaving the table.

In Lucian's private bathroom, I let my tears flow freely. I'm not surprised when the door open and Lucian's masculine frame fills the doorway. He steps inside, closing the door, and he holds me close until the waterworks come to an end.

"I'm sorry."

"Don't you ever apologize for loving me," Lucian commands. "Do you understand?"

I nod, emotionally drained and too shaken by my own thoughts to formulate a verbal response. Lowering his head, Lucian kisses my tearstained cheeks and swollen lips. In the safety of his arms, I feel strong again and ready for battle. He breaks the kiss, and I mourn the loss.

"Let's go home," he whispers against my lips.

I don't remind him that it's only twelve o'clock in the afternoon and his workday has barely started.

We leave his office with Thorne security shielding us from the paparazzi. Franklin pulls away from the curb into lunchtime traffic and William follows us.

Now that we're home the frustration and anger is more prevalent in Lucian. He held it together while we were at the precinct. And he didn't let anyone but me see him struggling for control while we were at his office. He's on the edge of losing that battle and I don't know how to help him.

"You can't control the world, Lucian."

He turns to me, his eyes dark with rage, but when he pulls me into his arms his touch is gentle and loving.

"No, but I should be able to keep bullshit away from you," he says, resting his forehead on mine.

Idly, I glide my fingers down the length of his tie. I want to comfort him, but most of all I want to remind him of an essential part of himself. A man in control.

Then it occurs to me that I can. With steady fingers, I loosen the knot in his tie before pulling it from around his neck. Placing the tie in his hand, I lift my wrists up to Lucian. His questioning gaze meets mine.

"You can't control the world," I repeat. "So, control what you can. Me." The rage in his eyes morphs into desire. "Control me," I whisper, my voice filled with need. "You have my submission."

"Rose Petal," he groans. "I don't know if I can be gentle." His confession only makes me want him more. "I need you too much."

"Take what you need," I urge. "You want to tie me up and spank me. Do it. I'm yours and I'll always give you what you need. Right now, what you need most is to reclaim the control the world is trying to steal from you."

He says nothing for a moment. Then he takes my hands, pressing his lips against my palms. "I want you in our bedroom stripped down for me."

"Yes, Sir," I say.

Lucian releases my hands and I walk away. I can feel his heated gaze following me.

In the bedroom, I undress, taking my time, letting each article of clothing fall from my body. Then I ready myself for Lucian. When the bedroom door opens, my head is bowed and I'm kneeling. My hands are resting flat on my thighs. And I'm only wearing red lace panties.

Lucian walks into the bedroom, closing the door behind him. My body hums with energy. The air around us somehow becomes charged. The atmosphere in the room magnetizes, drawing us closer. In that moment, comprehension of what we truly are to each other becomes clear. I am his and more importantly he is mine. A sense of peace comes over me, banishing any lingering doubt or fear. What we have is undeniable, always and forever.

With my head bowed, I could only see his shoes. I want to look up, to see the look in his eyes. Have I pleased him with my submission? I hope so.

He steps to me, and my heart races when he strokes my cheek. His touch is gone before I can lean into it.

"Is this what you want, Avery?"

"Yes, Sir."

Without saying another word, Lucian walks away.

I wait for him, and the longer I wait the anticipation grows. My breathing has become harsher, and the yearning is devouring me second by second.

When Lucian returns, I can't resist the urge to sneak a peek. I take a quick look and I am pleased to find him gloriously naked. I lick my lips hungrily, wanting the taste of him on my tongue. My center clenches, dampening my panties.

"Do you see something you like?" Lucian asks when he catches me staring.

"Yes, Sir, I do." Everything below my navel begins to clench and unclench.

"What's your safe word, Avery?"

"Lighthouse, Sir," I say, no longer looking away from him.

"Use it if you need to."

He offers me his hand, helping me to my feet. "I want you at my mercy."

I moan, and the desperate plea is undisguised and unapologetic.

"Give me your other hand, Rose Petal."

Giving Lucian my hand palm side up, I hold them together. I watch Lucian bind my wrists with his tie. His fingertips brush my skin, as he knots the blue tie that matches his eyes perfectly. Securing me firmly, the silk is soft against my flesh.

Lucian takes a step back, surveying his handy work. His lustful gaze rakes over my body. The heat from his hypnotic stare melts me.

"You're so fucking beautiful," he whispers, lifting me in his arms.

We are nose to nose when Lucian sinks his teeth into my bottom lip.

His words and a literal bite of pain have me craving more.

"And so goddamn fuckable," he groans, as he lowers me onto the bed.

"Lay on your stomach. I want your ass in the air."

I get into position, waiting for his next command. The bed dips when Lucian climbs onto it behind me. He pulls my hips to him, sliding my panties down to my knees. When I feel the length of his cock against my ass, it's hard and hot, warming me from the inside. The next sensation I feel scorches my soul.

Lucian's tongue glides down the seam of my ass, teasing my pucker. The bad things he does to me, torments and pleases me like nothing I've ever known. I writhe against his mouth, frantic for him to put out the fire he has caused. My pleas are answered when Lucian squirts lube in my ass, followed by his thumb. I cry out, in pain, in relief, in pleasure.

"Do you want more?" Lucian groans.

"Yes, oh please, yes," I beg.

Thrust after thrust, Lucian's thumb claims my ass, pushing me closer to my release. Abruptly he pulls out, leaving me empty. This time I cry out in frustration. Moments later, dissatisfaction is replaced by gratification, the emptiness replaced with a butt plug filling my ass. And I almost lose my fucking mind, the pleasure so intense I can barely contain it.

"Let go, Rose Petal. Just feel it." Lucian's deep lustful voice curls my toes.

The penetrating force of my orgasm quakes my body. I scream, unable to contain the tide of emotions flowing through me. Lucian spanks me, cheek after cheek, until I'm coming so hard an explosion of pleasure consumes me.

"I'm going to fuck you now."

Lucian places his hand on my lower back, pushing me down onto the mattress. He enters me from behind, leaving the butt plug in. The double penetration made more intense by my panties keeping my legs trapped.

"Fuck," Lucian growls. "You're so tight."

Clenching and unclenching around his cock, I squeeze him tighter.

"Again," his gentle command whispers against my ear.

I do as I'm told eagerly, his pleasure mine to give and take. Lucian pulls out, leaving only the head of his cock inside me. He pushes back into me with a deep penetrating thrust, filling me completely. I try to push back against him, but he has me pinned. Fucking me into oblivion, the mattress squeaks and the headboard bangs against the wall, taking a pounding as fiercely as I am. I've given him the right to take me this way, the way he wants to. The way he needs to.

"Look at me," he commands.

I meet his gaze over my shoulder. When Lucian leans in to kiss me, it takes my breath away. The gentleness of the kiss is a striking contrast to the aggressive fucking I'm receiving. His lips move to the shell of my ear, and he whispers, "You're mine." I want to shout 'hell yes' from the fucking rooftop, but my voice is crying out in an explosive never-ending orgasm. Chasing his release, Lucian's body trembles against mine, groaning, filling me with his seed.

He collapses, resting the weight of his body on mine for a moment. Rolling over onto his back, he pulls me with him. Loosening the knot from the tie, Lucian frees my wrists. I don't know how long I lay in his arms before he speaks.

"How do you feel?"

"Well fucked and tremendously loved."

"Me too," he whispers.

I know sex doesn't solve our problems, but for now it will do. For now, Lucian and I are all that matters.

Chapter 14
Lucian

AVERY AND I STAYED in bed yesterday until sunset, making love until we were all that existed. When we were finally able to let each other go, it was time for dinner. The new day seems brighter and full of possibilities because of her. I know we still have a lot of bullshit to deal with, and we will do it together. Having breakfast with Avery is the second-best way to start the day. The first is having Avery for breakfast, of course. Leaving her is never easy, but I make the trek to my office at Thorne Tower. I'm ready for battle knowing I have her in my corner.

I'm not prepared for the visitor sitting in the reception area when I step out of the elevator. I'd rather escort her to hell than have her in my life any longer. She stands and waits for me to reach her. Ignoring her, I take my messages from Helen.

"You're going to want to hear what I have to say." Her shrill voice makes the hairs on the back of my neck stand on end.

"I doubt that." I counter.

"I'm willing to discuss an amical solution, but my offer is only good until the lawyers meet for discovery."

I look her up and down trying to figure out how I could have been so wrong about this woman. She has always had a bit of a crush on me since college. We were a part of the same study group. And we spent a lot of time together. I even considered asking her out, until I met her fraternal twin sister Camille, two weeks later. There was something about Camille that Samantha didn't have, and I was attracted to that. To Camille. The three of us started hanging out socially. I began to see Samantha as a friend, then later as a sister.

The year following Camille and Ian's deaths was the worst. Samantha was there for me in the beginning, until I pushed her away. Her presence was too much of a reminder that my wife had betrayed me. Too much of a reminder that Camille and Ian were never coming back to me.

I was still consumed with grief one year after their deaths. I wanted to drown myself in every debauchery known to man. When I ran into Samantha at a night club, I only saw Camille and I wanted to punish her for her betrayal and the pain she had caused me. One drink with Samantha led to many. That night is still a blur. The next morning, I woke up in her bed with a headache, and very little memory of the night before. I felt ashamed and I apologized repeatedly, telling her we had made a mistake and it never should have happened. She agreed, and we said our goodbyes. She moved away for two years but returned to New York a few weeks ago. Now she's trying to dismantle me by destroying my life and my reputation. That's not going to happen.

"Just a few minutes of your time is all I'm asking." Samantha's voice breaks the spell the past has put me under.

"We both know that's not true."

"Three minutes or fifteen million dollars. It's your choice." She smirks.

I walk past her, entering my office, and she follows me.

"Your three minutes have started. I suggest you say what you came to say."

Samantha takes a seat in one of the chairs in front of my desk. Crossing her legs, her short skirt crawls up her thighs, revealing more than I care to see.

"I have a proposition for you, Lucian...one I think will be mutually satisfactory for all parties."

I don't respond, so she continues.

"The only solution to your little problem is quite simple," she gloats. "You marry me."

I can't hold back the laughter that climbs from my throat. I'm still laughing when she speaks again.

"Marry me and the civil suit goes away." The eeriness of her tone gets my attention, ceasing my laughter. "You never gave us a chance, so I'm taking it by any means necessary."

"Samantha, love doesn't work that way. You can't force someone to marry you and think that it will resemble real love in any way."

"I'll make you happy and your affections for me will grow. It'll be hard at first. I hear the first year of marriage is always the hardest. But we'll get through it. We'll have a child, a little girl I think, and you'll be happy again."

She continues as if she hasn't heard a word I've said. How can she possibly think she could replace the family I loss? No one could.

"No," I say, "I will not marry you."

"You would rather risk losing your freedom and your money?"

"I'm not risking anything."

She stands, nodding as she removes an envelope from her purse and places it on my desk.

"You'll understand if I don't give you the customary two-week notice before resigning. However, I'll give you until we meet again with our attorneys to accept my proposal."

She walks over to the door, pausing before she leaves. Turning to face me, her dark eyes are filled with malice and contempt.

"What are you willing to risk losing, I wonder?" she asks sinisterly, before walking out.

The envelope Samantha left on my desk is an irritating reminder of her. Opening it, I read the letter inside. It's short and to the point. I quit. The resignation letter is written on her stationary and bears her signature. I send a quick email to Dave Willis, head of Human Resources, and Carter Lincoln, head of Thorne Security. Carter will handle revoking all of Samantha's security clearances and Dave will deal with her exit package. Although, I can't imagine anything is owed to her considering she's only been with Thorne Broadcasting Network for a short time.

A few minutes after the email is sent, I receive a call from Carter.

"I have an ID on the pap from yesterday," he says without preamble. "He took off when Franklin came after him. However, Franklin was able to get a photo. I ran it through Thorne Security's facial recognition software, and I got a hit."

"Who is he?" I ask when I'm able to get a word in.

"Clayton Fields. Ring any bells?"

"I've never heard of him."

"Clayton Lucas Fields was born thirty-two years ago to Jean and Clayton Fields Sr. The preliminary background check reveals that he moved to New York three months ago from

Jacksonville, Florida. He was dishonorably discharged from the marines six years ago, arrested for theft, aggravated assault, and breaking and entering since leaving the military."

I listen as Carter run down the list of charges, then something occurs to me.

"Did you say he's from Jacksonville, Florida?"

"That's right."

"Camille and Samantha are from Jacksonville. Their parents moved back two years ago."

"I know what you're thinking and I'm on it. If their paths have crossed here or in Jacksonville, I'll find it," Carter assures me.

"I know you will."

Carter gives me a few more details about Clayton Fields and confirms that Samantha's security clearance has been terminated. Ending the call, I return to clearing my schedule.

Wrapping up a conference call, my iPhone beeps, alerting me to an incoming message. I nearly drop my phone when I read the message from a phone number I don't recognize. The text and the images chill my bones as panic races up and down my spine. The message is foreboding, and the images are of Avery.

Do you think you can keep her away from me? I can get to her anytime I want, and time is running out.

Bolting out my office, I use my private elevator to ensure there are no stops along the way. Helen utters something to me, but I'm too distracted to make out the words. The elevator seems to be moving too damn slow, even though I reach the lobby in no time. Racing out the door, I'm curbside when

Franklin spots me running toward him. He's getting out of the car when I stop him.

"Get back in!" I shout, opening the back-passenger door. "I need to find Avery."

Franklin is behind the wheel and pulling up the GPS tracker for Avery's BMW. We've only gone two blocks before traffic stops, due to an accident involving a cab driver and a bike messenger. The bike is mangled but everyone appears to be fine.

Frustrated, I try calling Avery again. Five times in a row my call have gone to voicemail. I open the app, accessing the GPS on the BMW. She's at the library. I won't feel true relief until I see her and hold her in my arms. I call her bodyguard Mathers, also for the fifth time, and there's still no answer. The limo starts to move, and I try to ignore the fear gnawing at me. I watch the miles on the tracker vanish the closer I get to her.

The limo has barely come to a stop, when I leap out, running up the stairs of the Mid-Manhattan branch of the New York Public Library. I search frantically for Avery without any success.

I'm making my way to the information desk, when I literally run into her, knocking her down.

"Avery," I groan.

Helping her to her feet and into my arms. I cover her mouth, smelling the cinnamon on her breath before I taste it. Mathers pick-up the books she was carrying, then steps away to give us some space. She softens against me, wrapping her arms around my waist. The dread that has plagued me since receiving the text message slowly leaves me. Breaking the kiss, I put some distance between us to examine her more thoroughly.

"Are you alright?" I ask

"I'm fine," she laughs. "My butt will survive the fall."

"Do you have any idea how worried I've been about you?"

She frowns.

"I'm fine, Lucian, really. I've been here all morning and William has been with me the whole time. We silenced our phones when we entered the library."

"I called you five times and got no answer." I say to her before giving Mathers a pointed glare.

"What's wrong, Lucian? Why are you here?"

"Get your things," I command. "We're going home."

For a moment, I think she's going to argue with me, but she nods, and I follow her to retrieve her messenger bag and MacBook.

I usher her outside and into the back of the limo, instructing Mathers to follow us back to the penthouse.

"What's going on, Lucian?" Avery asks when we're underway.

Opening the text message and giving her my phone. "This," I say by way of explanation.

Avery's hand trembles as she swipes the screen viewing each photo. I know when she comes to the most disturbing photo. She's straddling me on the beach, just as she reaches her climax. Dropping the phone to the floor, Avery gasps, her eyes wide with shock. Covering her face, she begins to sob. I grab her up in my arms, holding her on my lap.

"Whoever is behind this, I promise you they'll pay dearly for it," I vow.

My thoughts go to the last words Samantha said to me as she was leaving my office.

'What are you willing to risk losing I wonder?' The words repeat on a loop in my head.

Chapter 15
Avery

MY TEARS CLOUD MY VISION and stain my cheeks. Lucian takes my hand leading me into the penthouse in a blurry haze. I shake my head, a feeble attempt at erasing the images of the photos burning my corneas and rendering me blind to anything else. It was foolishly irresponsible of me to make love to Lucian out in the open where anyone could see us. Now a moment I thought was just between us was shared with a nameless, faceless stalker. I cringe at the thought of someone having proof of our intimate moment and keeping it as a trophy.

We're in our bedroom behind closed doors before either of us breaks the silence. Lucian speaks first.

"Do you know what I see when I look at the photos? Passion." Lucian says, answering his own question.

"It's not what you see in the photos that upsets me. It's what the person behind the camera sees."

"Are you ashamed of us?" he questions.

"I'm front and center, on display for anyone to see," I snap.

"It's okay that we're madly in love, kiss like no one is watching, and embrace each other like it'll be the last time, every time. That's passion and there's nothing to be ashamed of."

"I'm not ashamed. I'm angry. Angry at myself for being such a fool, believing that I can have you and the rest of the world doesn't matter. And I'm angry because some creep has a photo of my passion for you.

God only knows what it'll be used for."

Lucian frowns, as if an unpleasant thought has occurred to him.

"I'll find who's doing this," he promises.

I'm not sure he can keep that promise. Someone is targeting me. I know it and so does he. And we have no real proof that ties Samantha to any of this.

• • • •

FIVE DAYS AFTER LUCIAN received photos of us making love on the beach in East Hampton, I awake with a sense of foreboding. Alone in bed with the curtains drawn, it casts a gloomy spell over the room. Lucian and I made love throughout the night, knowing the morning will separate us. His business trip to Los Angeles will take him away from me for two days. We haven't been apart since those four days weeks ago, when his jealousy threatened to end us before we barely got started. The vivid memory of makeup sex sends a tremor through me. But that was foreplay compared to last night. My body aches deliciously where he has touched me. My lips are still kissed swollen. My nipples, clit, thighs, and hips are sore from being licked, sucked, and bitten all night. And my center is filled with the warmth of his seed. He has left behind this pleasurable pain as a reminder. With every breath I will feel Lucian, want him and miss him.

Smiling into the empty room, my heart overflows with joy at the words he whispered in my ear before leaving this morning. "Wear my collar while I'm away. To remind you that you're mine." Then he clasps it around my neck before kissing me goodbye.

The diamond choker wasn't given to me as a collar, but that's what it has come to represent; something tangible that says I'm his. I don't need to wear the necklace to remind me that the commitment we share is real. And I don't mind indulging his dominant needs, because just as surely as I am his, he is mine.

Climbing out of bed, I walk gingerly to the bathroom, my body not quite ready for the movement. I take a quick shower and dress before having breakfast. I'm seated at the breakfast bar when Maggie compliments me on my necklace.

"That's a beautiful necklace," she says, and I immediately feel overdressed.

Clad in dark skinny jeans, a classic white button-up shirt and red pointy ballet flats, the diamond choker rest slightly at my throat.

"Thank you," I say, self-consciously, lifting my hand to the necklace. "It was a gift."

Maggie smiles knowingly, giving me a nod, before resuming her work in the kitchen. I finish my breakfast in silence, reading over my notes for an upcoming article I'm writing for The New York Times.

Padding down the hall to the master bath, I brush my teeth for the second time this morning, before applying lip gloss. Pouting my lips, the image in the mirror is funny, yet extremely provocative, and I can't resist the urge to share it with Lucian. I take a few quick selfies and send them to him with a text that says, *I miss you already.*

William is waiting for me in the foyer when I return. He greets me cordially, escorting me to the elevator. He's rounding the front of the BMW, when I receive a text from Lucian. Just two words, a soft moan escapes and my body reacts instantly.

Soon, Sweetness.

We're exiting the garage and suddenly a loud crash jolt me forward. A white delivery van has plowed into us, hitting the front of the BMW.

"Are you okay?" William asks, unbuckling his seatbelt.

"I'm alright," I assure him.

"Stay inside the vehicle," he cautions.

I nod, and he steps out of the car, locking me in. Someone climbs out of the van, approaching William. They exchange words, but I can't make them out. Seconds later, the back of the van swings open and William drops to the ground on one knee. I watch the scene play out in slow motion. The masked man towers over William and fires another shot. My reactionary brain is working overtime, to formulate a plan. A plan that will end with me surviving this.

Removing my necklace, I stuff it between the seat, as I'm placing a call to Lucian, but it goes to voicemail. I'm leaving him a message when the masked man bangs on the window.

"Get out of the car." His voice is muffled by the mask he's wearing and the glass window separating us.

William had the foresight to leave the keys in the car. I'm safe inside for now. The bullet proof glass will hold them off for a while, but not forever.

The smaller man walks up to the driver side window and places a small amount of putty like white substance on the door. I've seen enough action films to guess that it could be some type of explosive. Removing a cell phone from his pocket, he makes a call and speaks briefly before ending the call and shoving the phone back into his pocket.

"Get out of the fucking car. We won't ask again," he shouts, his voice a bit feminine.

"The police are on their way," I shout back. "You should go while you still can."

I pick up my phone again, this time to dial the police, only to hear a busy signal. That's when I notice the blinking red light; the building's fire alarm has been triggered. My one call had been to Lucian, and I pray he checks his voicemail soon.

Unlocking the door, I climb out of the vehicle. The big man wearing the mask uses a cable tie to bind my wrists together, before blindfolding me and shoving me into the back of the van.

"Duct tape her mouth," the small man orders.

"You don't have to do...!" I shout just as the tape covers my mouth.

The doors are slammed shut, locking me in the back of the van. I hear two more doors slam, and then we're moving. The van is in motion for a long time, during which a few thoughts come to mind. The obvious being, the building's security personnel must have seen something and called the police. But no one came to my aid. No one even entered the garage. My kidnappers were in and out of the garage within minutes. This leads me to believe that this is not random, it was meticulously planned.

I'm also positive that the small man is no man at all. I recognize the perfume she's wearing. The thing that worries me is, what are they going to do with me once they get what they want? I know I should be stricken with fear and panic, but the need to survive is stronger. I'll do whatever it takes to get through this.

The van comes to a stop, and I hear two doors open and close. The back doors of the van open next. I'm dragged out and I stumble to the ground. I feel the cool concrete beneath my hands, and the dry dusty air tells me we're in some sort of warehouse.

'On your feet!" the man shouts, pulling me up by the arm.

Once standing, he shoves me, and I bump into a chair.

"Sit down," he orders

I take a seat, and after a while the metal seat becomes uncomfortable. The urgent need to relieve myself poses an imminent threat to the bottom half of my attire. I squirm in the chair and mumble under the duct tape.

"What the fuck is your problem?" the man barks, snatching the tape from my mouth.

"I have to use the restroom."

He removes the blindfold but leaves the cable tie in place. I scan my surroundings, noting that all the windows are blacked out. The door is a short distance away. More importantly, the woman seems to have left. With only one kidnapper to contend with, this increases my odds of escaping.

"Make it quick," he says harshly, pointing to the door to my left.

I scramble to my feet, hurrying to the restroom before I have an embarrassing accident. With just a toilet and sink, the restroom is cramped and not very clean. I take care of business as best I can with the limited use of my hands. I look around the small space for anything I can use to aid me in my plan to escape. The room offers nothing, and disappointment creeps in, shaking my resolve.

The doorknob shakes followed by the man's voice from the other side. "Your time is up. Come out or I'm coming in."

The door opens, and before I have time to think about it, I lunge at him, putting all my weight behind me. With my hands clasped tight, I land a hard strike to his face. Stumbling back, he covers his bloody nose. Determined to fight my way out, I come up with a knee to his balls, followed by a blow to his head with my elbows. He falls to the ground shouting some expletives and I run like hell towards freedom.

I've only made it a few feet when the woman appears in front of me. She's not wearing shades and the ball cap anymore. Before I can utter a word, she shoots me in the thigh. I look down at the point of impact, where a dart has pierced my skin. Removing it, I toss it to the ground. I continue to advance towards the door to freedom. But with each step my limbs become heavier and my head spins. I lose control of my body and I'm falling, but the fall doesn't seem to end. I try to speak, but there's no sound. I'm moving again, but I'm not walking. My body crashes against a hard surface. I know there is pain, but I can't feel it.

Closing my eyes seems easier than fighting to keep them open. Then there's only darkness. Lucian has found me in the darkness before, I know he'll find me again.

My eyes open slowly, and the darkness greets me. Icy cold fear shoots down my spine, and the terror of waking bound in darkness paralyzes me once again. The darkness and isolation remind me of another time when I was held against my will. I try to shake off the grogginess that's confusing me and wreaking havoc with my insecurities. This is not like the last time, I tell myself. I'm not what they want. I'm just the bait. But that also makes me disposable.

I don't know how much time has passed, but I need water and food. My mouth is dry and my stomach pangs with hunger. And I have a splitting headache, no doubt a side effect of whatever was used to tranquilize me. I yell as loud as I can to get their attention.

The door of the van yanks open and there she stands, the fucking lunatic who refuses to take no for an answer, Samantha Davies.

"Keep your mouth shut, bitch. Don't make me hurt you because I will. So, shut the fuck up."

"I need food and water," I say, ignoring her tirade.

She looks at me with disdain and steps away briefly. Returning with a crumpled bag, she tosses it to me and walks away again.

I manage to open the bag. Inside there's a cold sandwich and a warm bottle of water. Biting into the sandwich, I eat enough to stave off hunger but finish the water.

Samantha has left the van door open, allowing me to hear their conversation clearly.

"Do you think Thorne will pay the fifteen million to get her back?"

"He will if he wants her back in one piece." Samantha's cruel tone suggests she would be fine either way.

"I just want my cut," the man says.

"Is that all you want?" Samantha asks. Her attempt at seduction sounds insincere even to my ears.

I listen quietly to them discussing how they intend to spend Lucian's money. When the conversation turns toward them leaving town together, Samantha suggests they travel separately, so as not to draw any suspicion to themselves.

"You know I'm being followed," she reminds him. "I don't want to make any mistakes, now that I'm so close to getting what I want."

"What we want," he corrects her.

"Yes, of course. What we want."

The warehouse is silent for a moment, then I realize they're kissing. A faint giggle followed by footsteps tells me they have moved some distance away from the van.

Now that they have given me a distraction, I intend to free myself. Using my teeth, I pull on the cable tie making it tighter. Centering the ratchet between my wrist, I lift my arms to my chest, bringing them down, forcefully hitting my hipbone, by pushing my shoulder blades back. I attempt this several times, freeing myself on the fourth attempt.

Once again, a chance for freedom presents itself. I remove my shoes and run as fast as I can to the door. Distress sucks the air from my lungs, when I reach the door only to find it securely locked with a heavy-duty steel chain and a padlock. Not to be deterred, I look around for another escape route. The windows, although blacked out, presents another opportunity. But they are too high for me to reach. I run back to the van and grab the metal chair before heading to the windows. Climbing onto the chair, I can clearly see that the windows have been covered with a black peel and stick film. As luck would have it the film has started to peel away around the edges. Removing a large enough section, I am able to see outside. It's still daylight, but there's no one around as far as I can see. I continue removing as much of the film from the window as I can. Defeat breaks my heart at the sight of the metal window screen mesh. The reality of my situation is too painful to bear. I climb down from the chair and walk back to the van. The evidence of my escape attempt is left behind. Sitting in the back of the van, I put my shoes on, and I wait.

Chapter 16
Lucian

I WAS ON THE GROUND at LAX for thirty minutes before I notice the missed call from Avery. Returning her call, it goes straight to voicemail. I try calling two more times before listening to the message she left me.

"I think I'm about to be kidnapped. Two men, white delivery van inside the garage. One is wearing a mask. The smaller man is wearing a ball cap and shades covering most of his face. I can't make out the name on the van, but the license plate is New York GAL 0927. William has been shot; I think he's dead."

I can't fucking believe what I'm hearing. Playing the message again I hear what sounds like an exchange with Avery's abductor.

"The police are on their way," she shouts. "You should go while you still..."

The phone goes dead and there's nothing, but a gaping empty hole left in its wake, threatening to suck me into a pit of anger and despair. I struggle with the violent rage consuming me, holding it back with the sheer force of will and my love for the woman who has been taken from me. I'm no good to Avery if I let hate cloud my judgement. There will be time for vengeance after I've gotten her back.

I race back to my Gulfstream G650, instructing Wes Montgomery, my pilot, to takeoff immediately.

"Change of plans, I need to get back to New York immediately."

"Yes sir," Wes replies, correctly sensing the urgency and reacting accordingly. He hurries to the cockpit preparing for takeoff.

Taking a seat, I buckle up for the ascension. Placing a conference call to Carter, Franklin, and Jake, I apprise them of Avery's kidnapping.

"I'm on my way back to New York," I inform them. Meet me at the penthouse. I don't want this getting out before I have a chance to get ahead of it."

"Have the kidnappers contacted you yet?" Franklin asks

"No. And Jake, keep this from Raina until we know more."

Jake agrees, but the apprehension in his voice makes it known that he's not happy about keeping Raina in the dark.

"I've accessed the city's CCTV and I'm performing a citywide search. Starting at the time and place you've provided. Once I find a match to the license plate, I can track the van's movement. If I'm able to get a clear image inside the van, I will be able to run it through facial recognition to ID the kidnappers," Carter says.

"Connect me remotely," I instruct Carter. "I want to see everything you see."

I open my laptop, then wait impatiently for it to come to life. Once I've logged onto Thorne Security's mainframe, Carter takes over my laptop connecting me to the programs he's running. Images of Fifth Avenue come into view. The system scans quickly, searching the license plates captured by the CCTV.

"This could take some time," Carter cautions.

I hear the warning in his tone. He's trying to manage my expectations. What he doesn't understand is that Avery is my hope for everything and getting her back is the only option.

"Understood," I say, the one word conveying my own warning. "Do whatever it takes to find her. I don't care what it costs, just do it."

"That goes without saying," Carter replies. "I've sent a team to your place. And I'm checking for any reports of a shooting. Someone would have found Mathers lying in the garage by now and..."

"No need," Franklin interrupts. "I've just arrived, and the streets are barricaded for at least five blocks. I'm going to park the car and make my way to the garage. Check out the scene and find Mathers if he's still there. I will meet you at the airport in a few hours," Franklin confirms before leaving the conference call.

I would have preferred that he stayed connected, but I know he will be more effective if he doesn't have to contend with his phone.

"Emergency services reports receiving a bomb threat. The call came in about forty minutes ago. The caller gives your address as the location of the bomb," Carter says.

"It doesn't take a genius to figure out that whoever took Avery called in the bomb threat and used the chaos of the evacuation to go unnoticed," Jake surmises.

A fucking distraction. Avery has been heavily guarded the last few weeks. It would take putting Mathers down and something like this to get to her. But the guilt of leaving her behind tightens my chest, threatening to suffocate me from within.

"I'll be fine," she said last night cradled in my arms after we made love. "We aren't joined at the hip Lucian. Sometimes we'll need to do our own thing, apart from each other. And that means you take your business trip alone and then you come home to me as soon as you can."

I didn't push because I knew she was right. No matter how much I may want to, we can't spend every minute of the day together. We both have obligations that require our attention. But fuck, my first obligation should have been her. I should have made sure all threats had been dealt with before leaving her alone. I should have insisted she come with me because of the threats, or I should have fucking stayed in New York with her. I was only going to be gone for the day, cutting a two-day trip in half. I'd planned to take the jet home as soon as the meetings were done. I would have been back in her arms before midnight. I don't know how long I'm lost in my thoughts before the sound of Jake's voice reaches me. And the jolt of the plane moving forward reminds me that I still have a few hours to go before we land.

"Have you tapped into my building's security footage of the garage?" I ask Carter.

"I have, and the cameras are inconveniently blacked out. There's no footage of the area where your cars are parked."

"Are we still tracking Samantha's movements? Has she been anywhere near Avery or our home?"

"The last report has her at home since last night."

"Send whoever is watching her to her door. Make sure she's there."

"Enzo Delgado is assigned to her. I'm giving him a call now," Carter says.

I listen as Carter relays the instruction to Delgado. And we wait as he makes his way to Samantha's apartment. Delgado is a NYPD cop who moonlights with Thorne Security to pay for his daughter's tuition at Harvard. A good cop and an even better man. Hardworking and loyal. Never missed a day in the three years he's worked for me.

"NYPD," I hear Delgado say clearly. Carter has placed the call on speaker.

"How can I help you officer?" a female voice that does not belong to Samantha asks.

"I'm here to see Samantha Davies. Is she in?" Delgado asks.

"She's not here. And if you have any more questions, I want to see your badge." The woman is curt, but she has confirmed that Samantha is not at home.

Before I can voice an inquiry, Delgado begins interrogating the woman.

"How long has she been gone?" he asks. "When do you expect her back?"

She must have been satisfied with seeing his badge, because her next statement opens a floodgate of information.

"She left last night. Asked me to stay in her apartment for 24-hours. Said she was trying to get away from a controlling ex and she needed him to think she was at home. She told me to bring a wig the same color as my hair. I'm an actress, so I figure any paying gig is a good gig, you know. And she paid cash up front. Said she didn't want him tracking her credit card. "Is she okay? Is she in some sort of trouble?" the woman asks, finally taking a breath.

"I'm not at liberty to say, ma'am. I'm investigating a crime and all I can tell you is that Ms. Davies is a person of interest.

Any information you can give me regarding her whereabouts would be extremely helpful."

"You can call me Dana. That's my name. Dana Miller." She giggles. "And I don't know where she is right now. But last night after she made me switch clothes with her, she left in a white Zippy Express van. You know that express delivery company. The one with the corny slogan. We'll get it there in a zippy."

That fucking name again; the same courier company that delivered the threatening note to Avery. I know there is a connection. The pieces just aren't falling into place fast enough.

"I know it," Delgado replies.

"I remember thinking it was odd because they don't use the white vans no more. Not since that lawsuit a year ago when they had to change the logo. Something to do with copyrights. And when they changed the logo, they changed the van color to blue. But like I said, it was odd seeing the white van."

"You didn't happen to see who was driving the van, did you?" Delgado continues his questioning.

"No, it was too dark. I could only see that it was a man."

"Was Miss Davies forced into the van?" Delgado asks.

"Not unless kissing got a new meaning overnight."

Delgado chuckles a bit and then thanks the woman for her time. I hear footsteps as he walks away.

"Linc, did you get all that?" he asks Carter, referring to Carter by the nickname he earned with the Navy Seals.

"Hey, Officer Delgado," the woman calls out. "Samantha has my backpack."

"There's not much I can do about that, Miss Miller," he tells her.

"No, what I mean is she also has my cellphone; it's in my backpack."

"I don't follow," Delgado admits

"My phone has a GPS tracker. My sister downloaded an app on our phones, so we can keep tabs on each other. A girl can't be too careful in a big city like New York, you know. As long as my phone is charged you can track it."

"What's your phone number and the name of the app you're using?"

Delgado repeats the information back to the woman, but I'm sure it's for Carter's benefit. He thanks her again. But there is nothing but silence until the sound of a door closing.

Carter is the first to speak. "We heard everything, Enzo. Head over to Zippy Express, find out if there's a connection between Clayton Fields and anyone who works there that may have access to the old vans. Call me the second you have something. Leave no stone unturned."

"I'm on it," Delgado replies before ending the call.

I feel relief at the possibility of being able to track the woman's phone. Samantha is smart, so she would have gotten rid of anything that she had taken from the woman. Smart enough to know to stay off the grid until she's ready to make her next move. I know in my gut that Samantha has taken Avery. And the fact she has not contact me for a ransom only proves that she is not after my money, only my suffering. She knows I would never risk losing Avery. She's using my love for Avery against me. She's under the impression that loving Avery is my weakness. On the contrary, it gives me strength and purpose.

"I have a location on Miss Miller's cell phone," Carter says, and a kernel of hope grows inside me.

"Where is it? Where's Samantha?" I ask, sure that Samantha is responsible for Avery's kidnapping. My palms become sweaty waiting for Carter's response, hoping this is the break I need to find Avery sooner rather than later.

But the harsh intake of breath is all I need to hear. Whatever he has to say it's not good for Avery.

"The GPS coordinates place the phone at a diner in Brooklyn fourteen hours ago. I'm pulling up the satellite image of the area."

The image of the diner appears on my screen. Carter begins to zoom in on the image and pans the surrounding area. The neighborhood looks a bit rundown and abandoned buildings line most of the street. There are a few warehouses, most likely the reason why the diner is one of the few establishments still open for business.

"Check out the CCTV footage in the area since last night until the time the signal was lost on Miss Miller's phone," I instruct. "And meet me at the penthouse with whatever usable information you've gathered."

"I'll be there," Carter assures me, before dropping the line.

"Jake," I call, knowing he's still on the line with me.

"I'm here." His voice is reassuring, offering whatever support I need with just two words.

"I can't lose her." Fear chokes the words out.

Dread and fear boil in my gut, heating my blood like molten lava at the thought of Avery at the mercy of another kidnapper. What must she be feeling? The anguish she must be going through, reliving the memories of her abduction ten years ago. I shudder to think that she has been harmed in any way.

Heaven have mercy on the motherfuckers who took her because I won't.

"You won't lose her." Jake reaches in and pulls me out of the darkness. "You have the best fucking security team on the planet. And we both know Carter will find that needle in a haystack every god-damn time."

His words offer little comfort, and nothing will until I have Avery in my arms again. I can't lose the one person in this world I can't live without. The one person I love, crave, and need more than air.

But Jake is right. My security team is one of the best in the country, thanks to Carter. I know with his expertise I will find Avery.

"You're right. We will find her." I say, breathing truth and determination into the words. "But why the fuck haven't I heard from the kidnappers?"

I know in that moment that I would give anything, promise anything, and do anything to have her back safely with me. No amount of money is too much, and no sacrifice too great. What Avery has given me is priceless and irreplaceable.

"You will. And when you do, they will have underestimated you. They don't realize the lengths you're willing to go to, to get Avery back. And what you're willing to do to anyone who harms her."

"It's just that she's..." I stop myself from completing the statement.

"I know," Jake says. "Raina told me enough of what happened to Avery ten years ago."

The line is silent for a moment. When Jake speaks again, it's to remind me that Avery is no longer the scared fifteen-year-old girl who was sold to a sadistic son of a bitch, who raped and tortured her for weeks.

"Don't forget, she was calm enough to give you as much information as she could to find her. And you will find her," he repeats.

"Thanks," I say

"Why are you thanking me? I haven't done anything."

"You just reminded me that my girlfriend is badass."

And even if this is freaking her the fuck out, she'll handle it. At least that's what I tell myself.

"Let's just say that with all her self-defense training, I wouldn't want to be on her bad side."

I chuckle at the thought of Avery kicking her kidnappers' ass. Then the moment of joy fades when I remember what she told me the day she thought someone was following us.

'It gets to me sometimes, knowing that someone is watching me. How can I protect myself when I can't see the threat coming?'

All the security measures I've put in place didn't stop her from being taken. The kidnappers still found a way around the cameras in the garage and her bodyguard. No fucking way are they getting around me. I'm coming for her, and then I'm coming for them, whoever they may be.

"The plane will be landing soon," I tell Jake. "I'll see you at the penthouse."

"I'll be there," he says, repeating Carter's words before ending the call.

• • • •

THE JET TAXIS THE RUNWAY of the private airport coming to a halt at a waiting limousine. From the window, I see Franklin, Carter, Jake, and Marcus stepping out the limo.

All professionally dressed. All with a blank expression on their face. But Franklin's slightly slumped shoulders carry the strain of worry. I know it's due to the fragile girl we found abused ten years ago.

Exiting the plane, I climb down the steps and Franklin moves toward me. Closing the distance between us, he takes my bag. Now that we are face-to-face, I can tell by the intensity of his gaze that there has been a new development.

"What is it?" I ask.

Franklin tilts his head toward Carter as he approaches us.

"Carter will fill you in," he replies.

Whatever it is, I know without a doubt I'm not going to like it.

"I thought you would want to have this information as soon as possible," Carter says, as he hands me a file.

Taking the file, I open it to the first page. It's the police report of the day Camille and Ian were killed. My brows arch in confusion.

"Take a look at page four," Carter says.

Flipping the sheets of paper, I reach page four. Written across the page is a black question mark.

"That's the driver of the SUV original statement." Carter answered my unspoken question. "Read the section I've highlighted."

My heart stops when I reach the words 'the driver was speeding toward me and the next second she's jumping out of a moving car.'

"What the fuck does this mean?" I snap.

"The driver of the SUV, Tom Langdon, believes that Samantha deliberately caused the accident by speeding on the wrong side of the road and crashing into his vehicle," Carter explains

"The driver of the SUV was taken to the hospital. And later, when the police tried to question him, he claimed he couldn't remember anything."

"That's true. Initially he didn't remember the crash. When he began experiencing PTSD, Mr. Langdon sought help from a therapist. He recalls the accident as if it had just happened. He hoped that by going to the police and giving a statement, it would help somehow."

I take another look at the statement, and it's dated one year after the accident.

"Did the police question Samantha after receiving Mr. Langdon's statement?"

"The next page is a call log. They made three attempts."

The call list indicates that the first attempt was the same day the statement was given. The next attempt was the day after, which was also the day I woke up in her bed. The final attempt was made after she had moved to Los Angeles.

"There's another statement from Samantha attached also," Carter adds.

I anxiously turn the pages to get to Samantha's statement. I note that her statement is dated a week ago. The timing coincides with the civil suit and me being questioned by the police. Her statement alleges that she didn't tell the whole truth about the accident. It states that Camille and I argued, and I came after them, threatening to kill Daniel and Camille for betraying me. It further states that she lost control of the car, hitting the oncoming SUV, because I was pursuing them to take my son away from Camille. Then she lays the blame at my feet for causing the accident, killing my wife and son.

"There's no CCTV footage to corroborate either statement, but after interviewing, Mr. Langdon, my gut tells me that the man is telling the truth."

"When did you speak with him?"

"Before coming here," Carter answers. "The initial report didn't include Mr. Langdon's or Samantha's statement. With the police investigating you, I just assumed they updated the report after meeting with you last week."

"It also explains why it wasn't in Jake's copy." I add.

I don't know how to wrap my head around the fact that Samantha may be responsible for the deaths of my family. Her own sister and nephew. It's true that Samantha has always been a little jealous of Camille. But to purposely plow into an oncoming SUV and jump out of a moving car is insane to say the least. Then there's the move to Los Angeles, leaving New York before she's questioned by the police. That's odd, considering how torn up she professes to be about losing her twin sister and nephew. Now, two years later, she's trying to destroy my world again. I won't let it happen.

We climb into the back of the limo, leaving the airport behind.

"I'm here for whatever you need," Marcus says, breaking a long silence.

I meet his gaze, grateful for his support, but confused as to why he's here.

"You said not to tell Raina," Jake chimes. "You said nothing about telling Marcus."

From the sandbox to the graveyard, I say to myself. These are the men who will walk through hell and back with me. The men who are more than just lifelong friends, they are my family.

When we reach the penthouse, we're greeted by William Mathers. He approaches me the moment I step out of the elevator.

"I found him in the garage," Franklin says. "He'd been shot twice with a tranquilizer, but he's refused medical attention."

"Mr. Thorne," Mathers says. "I'm here to help find Miss West and get her back, sir." His military training is evident in his tone and posture. His former career as a navy seal is one of the reasons Carter recruited and then hired him.

"Tell me everything that happened," I say, indicating that he should follow me.

Mathers starts from the beginning, filling in the blanks before Avery's voice message. He also confirms that the driver of the van was Samantha Davies.

"She tried to conceal her identity with a ball cap and shades," Mathers says. "I recognized her almost immediately. But before I could remove Miss West from the situation, a masked man jumped out the back of the van. After that, total darkness, until Franklin was standing over me in the garage."

"You don't know what drug was used to take you down. You should be at the hospital getting checked out," Franklin advises.

"I'm not going anywhere until we get Miss West back," Mathers snaps

Franklin nods, when he sees the same resolve in Mathers eyes as I do. He has lost men in his long military career. And Avery being taken on his watch is eating at him. I will use that determination and dedication to my advantage.

"Has that cell phone come back on?" I ask, directing my question to Carter.

"No. But we showed a photo of Samantha to the owners. They confirm that she was at the diner last night and again this morning."

"What time this morning?"

"About five hours ago."

"So, what are we waiting for? They have to be held up somewhere nearby."

"That was my assumption," Carter states. We're checking out the warehouses in the area, but so far nothing."

"Someone had to have seen her."

"Unfortunately, CCTV was a dead-end. The cameras in the area are practically nonexistent."

Mathers walking away gets my attention.

"You have somewhere else you need to be?" I bark.

"Yes sir," he says, turning to face me. "The diner. If the kidnappers have Miss West in the area, it's a safe bet that they're getting their meals from the diner. I'm going to stake out the diner until Samantha returns and then I'm going to follow the bitch back to Miss West."

"Not without me."

"This needs to be a solo op, sir. Too many vehicles, too many boots on the ground will draw unwanted attention."

"That's not an option. I'm coming with you. Any other suggestion?"

Mathers studies me intently. And I can only assume he saw what he needed to see, just as I had with him earlier.

"We go without the extra security, without the limos and the suit and tie. We don't want to stand out," he says. "Carter and the rest of the team can provide support from a distance. We still need the intel they provide."

"There are a few things you're going to need," Carter advises.

"Just the basics," Mathers agrees. "I'll meet you back here in one hour."

"Everything you need will be here when you return," Carter assures Mathers, as he walks to the elevator.

It has been more than five hours since Avery was taken from me. Five hours since anyone has seen her. Five fucking hours she's been held captive, thrown back into a situation much like the one she endured ten years ago. And that is five goddamn hours too long. Avery is brave and strong, and one of the most resilient people I know. But she still has nightmares from the ordeal of that first kidnapping. I know it has got to be messing with her head. It's certainly fucking with mine. I make my way to our bedroom to be alone, while we wait for Mathers to return. Once I leave this room, I won't be stepping foot in it again. Not until Avery is back where she belongs.

Chapter 17
Avery

I AM NOT SURE HOW LONG I sit in the back of the van, after my failed escape attempt. Long enough that echoes from the past have begun to create fear and doubt. Fear that Samantha wants me dead because it's not about the money for her. She wants Lucian. And I'm beginning to doubt that Lucian will find me in time. However, never seeing Lucian again is what I fear most. I fear that the last time I said, 'I love you', was the last time.

The giggling of a woman who just faked an orgasm interrupts my desolate thoughts. I have no doubt that her screams were a performance, not only for her lover, but also for me.

"What the fuck?" I hear Samantha shriek. "She's escaped."

The sound of Samantha running, halts, when the man says, "Not possible."

Heavy footsteps approach the van. Within seconds, the man is standing before me.

"She's here," he assures Samantha. "But she has escaped the cable tie."

Samantha rounds the van and stands beside the man.

"Do you want me to shoot you again?" she sneers.

"Did you really think I wouldn't try to escape again?"

"Get the cable ties," she instructs the man. "Tie her up again."

"Don't bother. You've seen with your own eyes that I can get free of them. And I've seen that there's no escape. And no, I don't want to get shot with a tranquilizer again. So, I'll stay put and we'll wait this out."

"You say that like you have room to negotiate," the man laughs.

"I'm not the one you're going to have to contend with."

"Are you so sure Lucian will pay to get you back?" Samantha asks.

"I'm sure you'll pay for taking me." My confidence is returning. The doubt I had in Lucian is disappearing with each word.

"I see you believe the lies he's told you. My sister believed them too and they destroyed her."

Samantha's choice of words reminds me of the threatening note delivered to the penthouse weeks ago.

I tried to warn you, to give a chance to do the right thing. Next time I will be more direct. I will expose the truth and watch as the lies destroy you.

Any suspicion that I may have had about the note being from Samantha have been confirmed. Then it occurs to me that she may have had something to do with the accident that killed Lucian's wife and son. That's too impossible to believe. She would have been killed too had she not been thrown from the car. But is that how it happened? I've been through several self-defense courses that taught participants how to jump from a moving car. I see the moment she realizes I've made the connection. Her pupils dilate, and a sinister grin curls her lips. The bitch is truly bat shit crazy.

"A reckoning is coming, that's for damn sure," the man says. "And your boyfriend will pay one way or another."

"We need to prepare for the next step," Samantha states. "Leave her in the back of the van and lock the door."

The van doors slam shut, enclosing me in darkness. And I'm left alone once again. I sit quietly contemplating possible outcomes. From Lucian showing up and rescuing me, to me hotwiring the van, driving it through the chained door, rescuing myself. Of course, that would mean I would have to know how to hotwire it. Which I don't. I'll admit that if Lucian crashes through the door to save me, it will satisfy my action hero fantasy. I'm no damsel in distress, but sometimes a girl needs a hero; a champion who will slay her dragons. And Lucian Thorne is my dragon slayer.

"Get up," the voice shouts.

I can only assume that my inability to stay awake has everything to do with the tranquilizer. Since the back of a van is not where I would choose to take a nap.

"Go relieve yourself," he says, pointing the tranquilizer gun at me.

"Don't try anything or I will shoot you."

Climbing out the van, I walk past my kidnapper to the small restroom. When I'm done, I head back to the van. Sitting on the edge, I face him eye to eye. Now that he is no longer wearing a mask, the swelling across his nose, and the dark circles under his eyes is evidence that I've broken his nose.

"Samantha is using you," I say to him. "She's not doing this for the money. She wants Lucian."

"You think I believe a word coming out your mouth?"

"Did she tell you about the civil suit? She's suing Lucian for fifteen million dollars."

"Yeah, she told me. She thinks he'll buy his way out of it and get away with what he did to her sister and nephew."

I laugh. "Is that the lie she told you to get you to do all this for her?"

"What's so goddamn funny?" he barks

"Did she tell you that she proposed marriage to Lucian in exchange for dropping the civil suit? Does that sound like the actions of a woman who believes Lucian is responsible for the deaths of his wife and child? I think not. She's obsessed with him and has been for a long time."

I can practically see the wheels turning in his head. And the doubt manifesting itself. So, I attack his pride.

"She faked that orgasm earlier."

And there it is... the final nail in the coffin, so to speak.

"How the fuck...?"

"No woman experiencing a real orgasm speaks that clearly during the event," I say, cutting him off. "Especially if it's as good as she was pretending."

"You'd say anything to save yourself and that son of a bitch you call your boyfriend," he accuses.

"It's true I'd do almost anything to save myself from what Samantha has planned for me. But I don't need to lie to you when you already know the truth."

"What do you mean? What has she got planned for you?"

"She wants Lucian for herself and if she can't have him, no one can."

"Hell, no, that's not part of the plan. No fucking way am I committing murder."

Part of me is relieved that this man does not want to harm me. However, he still needs to be convinced that Samantha has a different agenda. So, I take a gamble and play a hunch.

"I heard Samantha call you Luke." It was more like she screamed it during her fake orgasm. Again, I'm sure that was for my benefit.

"Yeah," he confesses warily. "My middle name is Lucas."

"Lucian's friend used to call him Luc, in college. Samantha was one of those friends. I know it's hard to accept the truth sometimes. But if you look at the evidence, it's plain to see that Samantha has been dishonest with you all along."

"If all I can get out of this is the money, then so be it. I'll fucking disappear with my millions to some fucking island."

"Do you think she hasn't thought this all through? She lied to you because she needs a scapegoat. She's going to kill me, and you will take the blame for it."

"I'm not going to let that happen. We'll get the money and go our separate ways if that's what she wants, but I won't let her kill you." His words are so adamant, I almost believe him.

"Get back in the van," he orders. "Samantha will be back soon with food."

Climbing into the van, I'm surprised when Luke doesn't lock me in. He does, however, duct tape my mouth and zip tie my wrists again, before taking a seat on one of the three metal folding chairs. He stares at me with the eyes of a man who has been betrayed. But I don't feel sorry for him. He made the choice to kidnap me. He made the choice to shoot Mathers. Although, now I realize that Mathers had been shot with a tranquilizer just as I had. That eases my conscience a great deal. Believing that I was indirectly responsible for Mathers' death weighed heavily on my heart. He's a good man and deserves better.

For now, I wait. I wait for salvation or termination.

Chapter 18
Lucian

MATHERS AND I HAVE been waiting two hours across the street from the diner. Mathers' pickup truck is inconspicuous in the neighborhood. It's also a vehicle Samantha would not expect me or my security team to arrive in. Although my security team is strategically placed within a five-block radius, Franklin and Carter insist that we have backup. They warn me that it would be a mistake to think that Avery's kidnappers are working alone. And it would be an even bigger mistake to believe they aren't armed and dangerous.

When Mathers returns as promised an hour later, Carter had a small duffle bag ready for him filled with what they call the basics. The basics includes two nine millimeters semi-automatic handguns, ammunition, and binoculars.

With a deadline imposed by the ransom note I received via text thirty minutes ago, I'm running out of time, before I must meet the kidnappers' demands. One demand clearly states that I should come alone if I ever want to see Avery again.

"I can't stay here much longer," I tell Mathers. "I won't risk Avery's life, even if it's a safe bet."

He nods, understanding my plight.

"You do what you need to do. I have this covered," he assures me.

The kidnappers demand that we meet at the Carousel in Central Park. Once there, I'm to transfer the fifteen million dollars. The bank account number will be provided at the meet.

Carter assures me that once I've sent the money and have Avery back, he can retrieve the funds. I'm not worried about getting the money back. My priority is getting Avery back.

"I have a visual," Mathers says, lowering then raising the binoculars. "On the corner, female wearing a ball cap," he points out as he passes the binocular to me.

"That's her," I say, reaching for the door.

Mathers locks the doors, stopping me.

"We don't want to spook her," he explains.

"I need to make her take me to where she's holding Avery."

"She won't do that if she knows we're onto her. We will follow her."

I force myself to settle down, and to think more strategically.

"Carter," I call out over the speaker phone. "Did Miss Miller's cell phone come back on? Are you able to track it?"

Carter responds immediately. "Yes. I'm sending you the GPS coordinates now."

The coordinates appear on my screen, placing the phone in the exact spot as Samantha.

"We can keep a safe distance by following the GPS, not the woman."

A man of few words, Mathers nods in agreement.

We wait silently for ten minutes, our eyes glued to the entrance of the diner. Finally, Samantha steps out of the diner carrying a bag. Mather's hunch was correct. She appears to be getting her meals from the diner. Therefore, it stands to reason that Avery is somewhere nearby.

We follow the GPS, maintaining a two-block distance, since Samantha is walking. When the GPS signal is lost, and Samantha is nowhere in sight, I begin to panic.

"What the fuck!" I exclaim.

Mathers circles the block, seemingly ignoring my outburst. I check the screen again, hoping desperately the signal will reappear. I'm now down just thirty minutes before I need to leave to meet the kidnapper at the Carousel.

The pickup truck comes to a stop.

"What do you see?" Mathers asks, his eyes never leaving the sight ahead.

"Nothing. No one," I snap.

"I see a metal garage, metal screening on the windows, and most likely a concrete floor inside."

"What's your point? I don't have time for twenty questions, or I spy."

Mathers chuckles, but otherwise stares intently at the garage.

"It's a Faraday cage."

"A what?"

"Elevators and other rooms with metallic conducting frames can mimic a Faraday cage. This can lead to the loss of cell signals making it a 'dead zone' for cellphones, radios, and other electronic devices. They're in that building. I'd bet my life on it."

"No," I say. "You're asking me to bet Avery's life on it."

"It's your call."

If I leave now I'll reach the park on time. But I know Avery won't be there because my gut tells me she's here waiting for me.

"Let's go get my girl back."

"Do you know how the use one of these?" Mathers asks, offering me a nine-millimeter.

Accepting the weapon, I check the mag and the safety. My skills with weapons come from the tutelage of my uncle Jeremy. A summer spent with my cousin Julian and his father was both fun and educational.

"I do."

"The garage has one entrance. And I don't see any security camera."

"So, they won't see us coming," I finish.

"You ready for this?" Mathers asks.

My stomach clenches. The reality of what I'm about to do causes some anxiety. However, to get Avery back, I would gladly put a bullet through her kidnappers' fucking heads. And not think of them again. When anxiety gives way to anger, I give Mathers the okay.

Climbing out of the pickup truck, we approach the deserted garage. Mathers takes the lead with his firearm drawn. Backing him up, I remove the safety on my weapon.

As luck or fate would have it, we catch up to Samantha as she's entering the garage. We rush her before she has time to lock the door. Mathers grabs her from behind, covering her mouth. Samantha bites into his hand, and it falls away. She moves quickly, freeing herself.

"Clay!" she yells. "We have company. Bring our guest to greet them."

Movement in my peripheral draws my attention. And seconds later, Avery comes into view. Her mouth is covered with duct tape and her wrists are bound together with a cable tie. But her eyes tell me everything I need to know. They speak to me even when she can't.

I'm okay. I knew you would come for me. I love you.

Meeting her gaze, I give her my reply. It's just one word.

Always.

"I don't mean to interrupt such a lovely reunion," Samantha says as she walks over to Avery. Pointing her weapon at Avery, her eyes are trained on me. She doesn't seem to care that Mathers and I have guns aimed at her. She knows I won't risk firing a weapon, with her holding a gun to Avery's head. She knows she has me between a rock and a hard place.

We're out of options.

"Take their guns, Clay. They won't be needing them," she says to the man I now know is Clayton Fields.

Approaching us carefully, Fields orders us to put the guns on the floor and kick them toward him.

"Don't forget to search them for more weapons," Samantha says.

"You can't trust a man who shows up uninvited to break a date."

Fields pats me down first and finds nothing. He finds a small caliber gun in Mathers right boot.

"You should give this up while you still can," I say to them.

"We're not giving up a fifteen-million-dollar payday," Fields says.

"You can't possibly think you'll get away with this."

"I don't see why not. You're here, we can do the transfer and we can go our separate ways."

"You can't be that stupid," Mathers asserts.

"Need I remind you that we're the ones with the guns and the hostages," Samantha taunts.

"What do you want, Samantha? Money? Let Avery go, and you can have whatever you want. Just let her go," I plead.

"You don't mean that," she says.

"I do. I mean every word."

She laughs. "It's funny you should say those words. I do. When I proposed last week, you were the one doing the laughing."

I cringe slightly, realizing we've come full circle. I force myself to meet Samantha's gaze. And I tell her the truth.

"I'd do anything to keep her safe." I glance toward Avery. Her eyes glisten with unshed tears, and her hypnotic hazel gaze shines with love and trust.

"So, you'd risk breaking her heart to save her?

"I would," I answer, my gaze returns to Avery.

"You'd marry me to..."

"What the fuck, Sam? Is that what this has been about all along? You want Thorne for yourself?"

"I'm sorry Clay, but it's always been him."

"So, it's true. Everything Avery told me while you were out, it's all true."

"I've never loved anyone but him. I always knew we'd be together, I just had to remove the obstacles."

"You lying scheming bitch," Fields shouts. "Is that what the fuck I am to you... an obstacle... something to be disposed of?"

"You were a necessary evil. I couldn't have made my plan work without you. Gaining access to Lucian's penthouse and swapping out the cooking oils for peanut oil was all you."

"You've been setting me up all this time. Telling me lie after lie. Did he really kill Camille and her son?"

"Of course not."

"Did you kill them?" I ask, not expecting a confession, just a reaction.

She looks away, almost ashamed.

"I tried to save Ian, but I was too late," she begins, confessing how she has always loved me and that it should have been her not Camille.

"I wanted us to be a family. You, me, and Ian."

I can barely believe what I'm hearing. Rage blinds me as I step to her. Mathers reaches out, pulling me back by the arm.

"I saw you first," she continues. "And Cam just swooped in and took you away from me. I didn't mean for them both to die. I tried to save Ian for you. I wanted us to be a family," she repeats. "When I ran into you one year after their deaths, I knew it was a sign."

The memory of that night still evades me. And the next words from her deceitful mouth solves the mystery.

"So, after we had a couple of drinks, I drugged you. You would be surprised the things you can buy in the ladies' room of a night club," she quips. I was hoping to get pregnant, and we could start anew with a family of our own. But it wasn't our time yet. The police wanted to question me after the driver of the SUV regained his memories. Leaving town was my only option."

I lunge at Samantha, knocking her to the ground. The gun goes off and I spare a moment to see that Avery is okay. Knowing she hasn't been hurt gives me relief. For a split second, blinded by rage, I forgot to put her safety first.

A loud crash, followed by several footsteps, alerts me to the fact that we're no longer alone. I grab Samantha by the neck, pulling her to her feet.

"Let me go," she wails.

I squeeze tighter, crushing her throat. But a small voice stops me.

"Lucian." My rose petal approaches me, free from the duct tape and cable tie. Following closely behind her is Enzo Delgado.

"I can take it from here, Mr. Thorne," he says. Taking Samantha by the arm, he pulls them to her back. He begins reading her Miranda rights as he handcuffs her. "You'll both have to come down to the station to give statements," he advises.

Delgado takes Samantha away, leaving me alone with Avery.

"Are you okay?" I ask, brushing my lips gently over hers as I pull her into my arms.

"I'm okay," she tries to assure me. "I just want to go home."

We exit the garage hand in hand. Outside, there are several police cars as well as members of my security team. Mathers is speaking with Delgado and Franklin has just arrived, bringing the limo to a stop a few feet away from me and Avery. He exits the vehicle, rounding the front, he opens the back-passenger door. Avery slides in and I follow her. Moments later, we are leaving the scene behind. Avery is quiet, pressed against the door and staring out the window. I reach for her, taking her by the hand and she winces. Lifting her hand, I see the bruising caused by being bound with the cable tie.

"Come here, Sweetness," I beckon.

Avery slides closer to me, and I lift her onto my lap.

"Please forgive me," I beg. "I'm so sorry this happened to you because of me."

"You didn't do anything to cause this, Lucian."

"Samantha wanted to hurt you because of me."

"That isn't your fault." She lifts her head meeting my gaze. "And it isn't your fault what she did to your family."

I hold her tight, afraid to let her go. Afraid that she'll slip away.

We stay locked in a tight embrace for the entire trip back to Manhattan.

Taking the elevator up to the penthouse, we shut everyone and everything out. Tomorrow will be soon enough to face the world again. For tonight, in the sanctuary of our home, we'll exist only for each other. Tonight, we'll reinforce our undeniable bond.

• • • •

WHEN THE SUN RISES, I'm awake to greet it. A fitful night's sleep kept me awake most of the night. Samantha's confession has cut me to the core, reopening wounds I thought had healed long ago. And grief and agony cause me to feel like I've lost them all over again.

Avery is sleeping peacefully at my side now. However, last night she tossed and turned, crying out in her sleep. I held her close, preventing her from sleepwalking. Whispering words of love in her ear, she eventually settled into a deep and restful sleep. Once she awakes, the reality of yesterday's events will consume our day. Hours of police questioning, reliving the nightmare of yesterday, as well as three years ago.

Last night I desperately wanted to lose myself in her. Seeing the bruises on her wrist and the memory of my dead son was too much to bear. Knowing that one woman is the cause of so much devastation in my life is dismantling me from the inside. I also know that blaming myself is consuming me. I blame myself for not seeing how dangerous Samantha had become sooner. If I had, maybe my son would still be alive. Maybe Camille would be too. Although after her betrayal, our marriage would be over. Getting past this won't be easy and I don't know when we'll feel normal again. With Avery by my side, I know I have a chance at true happiness. We have a bond unlike any I've ever experienced. Loving her is as natural as breathing.

Closing my eyes, I breathe her in, giving in to her intoxicating scent. I welcome the peace and warmth of her body pressing against mine. A combination of exhaustion, exaltation, and Avery gives me what I need to surrender to sleep.

Nearly two hours after falling asleep, Avery stirs in my arms.

"Good morning," she murmurs as her lips brush against my pectoral muscles.

"Good morning, beautiful."

"I love it when you call me beautiful," she moans. "Like it's my name."

"I guess I've given you a few nick-names," I chuckle

"And you have a way of saying my name like it's a sexy dirty word." She moans again. "It's such a turn on."

The sound sends all the blood in my body directly to my cock, swelling it painfully.

"Avery," I whisper her name. My tone is seductive and filled with dirty intentions.

"Yes," she says.

I pull her leg over my hip, and she straddles me.

"Put me inside you, Avery," I order. "Now."

Her pupils dilating tells me that the command turns her on as well. Fisting my cock, she rests the bulbous head against her slick wet cunt. Teasing me, before sliding down my long hard shaft. I groan when she takes all of me in. She rides me vigorously, her breasts bouncing up and down is hypnotic. Lifting my hips, I thrust deep, hitting her G-spot. She cries out, clenching tightly around me.

"God, I love you," I practically growl.

"I love you too" she pants. Her breathless declaration fuels the already explosive passion I feel for her.

Pulling her down, her breasts press against my chest, I cover her mouth with mine. Kissing her feverously, I swallow her gasps and moans. Wrapping my arms around her back, I hold her close, thrusting deep into her body. She stiffens above me, nearing her orgasm. The sound of our desperate need for each other fills the room, chasing the release we denied ourselves last night. Avery detonates around me, triggering my own explosion. My seed flows from my body in long spurts, spilling into hers. Avery's sweet pussy tightens around me, milking every drop from me. Exhausted, I hold her until our breathing returns to normal.

"Dr. Hayes will be here soon to see you."

"It's really not necessary. I feel fine," she says

"You were drugged," I remind her. "I didn't press yesterday when you refused to go to the hospital, but this is nonnegotiable."

She sighs. And I feel the resistance tense her body.

"If you don't want to do it for yourself, do it for my peace of mind. I need to know that you're okay."

"Alright," she relents. Freeing herself from my hold, she climbs out of bed. "I should shower and get dress before she arrives."

I let her go without following her. Even with the orgasm, we are both still on edge. We're going to the police station to give our statements soon. Reliving the last twenty-four hours will be difficult. And unfortunately, I can't take that experience away from her.

Samantha will pay for all she's done.

• • • •

FOR THE SECOND TIME in a week, Avery and I are at the police station. They take us into separate interrogation rooms, keeping us apart, so we are not influenced by the information the other gives.

I give my account of the events, starting with the voicemail I received from Avery. The questions regarding Samantha's involvement in Camille and Ian's death are the hardest. Samantha's words rattle around in my head. *'I didn't mean for them both to die.'* It took Avery and every bit of self-control I possess not to strangle the life out of her.

After I've given my statement, Delgado grants my request to see Samantha. He leaves me alone with her, handcuffed to the large metal table separating us.

"You have five minutes," Delgado says before leaving.

That's all I need. If I stay longer, I may become physically ill.

"Was it worth it?" I ask. "Killing my family. Tormenting Avery. Only to end up here and alone."

She stares at me, silent for a moment.

"Would you have really married me to keep her safe?"

I don't acknowledge her delusion. Instead, I ask a question of my own.

"Did Fields keep copies of the photos he took of Avery and me on the beach?"

She laughs, and it sends a chill up my spine.

"Clay wouldn't know how to use a camera if it was a Polaroid One Step. He held the camera for show."

"If it was for show, why did he try to kill Avery with the peanut oil?"

"He hates you."

"That much I've gathered. But why? I've never met the man."

"Clay has been in love with Camille since high school. And when I told him you were responsible for her death; I could get him to do almost anything. I may have led him to believe you were the one with the peanut allergy."

"I see. He was trying to kill me."

"No. He only wanted to punish you."

"Why are you telling me all this? Hasn't your lawyer advised you to keep quiet?"

"Because I don't want there to be any secrets between us."

"There is no us," I snap.

She nods, seeming to accept my answer.

"I can pretend to be Camille and let you punish me. I've heard you're into that sort of thing. Of course, the one night we shared, I had to do all the work. I didn't mind. You were hard for hours. And I was so desperately greedy for you. I had you all to myself. I could touch you, taste..."

"That's enough!" I shout, cutting her off. "We're done here."

Turning my back on her, I walk to the door to leave. However, vengeance rears its ugly head, stopping me in my tracks. I turn around to face her.

"You could never pass as Camille. She was warm and loving, that's what drew me to her. You've always been a pale imitation."

Samantha's shocked expression is the closure I need. And this time I do leave. The time I spent with her begins to fade from my memory, the moment I see Avery standing in the hall.

She walks into my open arms. Wrapping her arms around me, she lets out a soft breath.

"Let's go home," she says. And they are the best words I've heard all afternoon.

Chapter 19
Avery

THURSDAY IS LIKE ANY other morning. I'm working from home. And Lucian is preparing to go to his office at Thorne Tower. I know the decision to return to work today was difficult for him to make. I've had nightmares for the past three nights and he's worried about leaving me home alone. I'm also aware that he's not sleeping well. And it's not because he stays awake to watch over me as I sleep. Managing to convince him that getting back to normal would help was not an easy task. The thing is, I'm not sure what normal is.

Lucian standing near the breakfast bar stops me in my tracks, when I emerge from our bedroom. A familiar electrical charge magnifies the closer I get to him. His form is impressive, even from behind. His lean muscular body fills his tailor-made charcoal gray suit perfectly.

Although I haven't made a sound or moved toward him, the way his body shifts imperceptibly tells me that he senses my presence. More than that, it tells me that he welcomes it.

"Good morning, beautiful," he says, before turning to face me.

"Good morning, sexy," I return.

He smiles, but it does not reach his eyes. I join him at the breakfast bar, taking a seat.

"I'll be home by six-thirty, but if you need me before then don't hesitate to call."

"I'll be fine. I have work to keep me busy. Raina is coming for lunch and there's a bodyguard outside the door."

"I worry Avery. I don't want..."

"I know. And I worry about you," I say, cutting him off. "That's why I think you should see Dr. Reynolds." He lifts his brow, but I ignore it and continue. "You need to talk to someone about the grief and the guilt you're feeling. I think Dr. Reynolds can help."

He stares at me for a moment as if he disagrees. Then he says,

"That's why I'm seeing her later today."

I love how self-aware he is. To know that he's struggling and is willing to accept help when he needs it.

"Okay," I nod

With the topic closed for now, Lucian gives me a kiss before heading to the door.

"I love you!" I shout after him.

He hears the need in my voice, and so do I. Swift, long strides bring him back to me. Pulling me from my seat, he wraps his arms around me. I can't hold back the moan that escapes when his mouth covers mine. The kiss is tender at first, as if seeking forgiveness. Then it changes; it's demanding and possessive, taking what is rightfully his. I feel my lips swelling under the pressure. It feels so good, I don't ever want it to end. We're breathless when Lucian ends our kiss.

His soft kiss-swollen lips brush against mine and he whispers, "I love you, Avery West."

With a satisfied smile, he releases me. And I can't help but notice how much brighter his eyes are.

I walk with him to the foyer, kissing him goodbye again before letting him leave. I head to my home office to get as much work done as I can before Raina arrives for lunch.

The morning hours have rolled seamlessly into the afternoon. When I finally take a break, I'm hungry and I need to pee. I pad down the hall to the bathroom, freshening up a bit before making my way to the kitchen.

When Raina arrives, I'm preparing a light lunch of soup and sandwiches. She joins me in the kitchen.

"Do you want some help?" she offers.

"You can grab our drinks from the refrigerator."

Retrieving the drinks, she asks, "How are you?" before taking a seat at the breakfast bar.

Raina was here two nights ago, when Lucian and I invited Katelyn, Marcus, Jake, and the Prestons over for dinner. We wanted to tell them about the kidnapping and Samantha's involvement in Camille and Ian's deaths, before the media got wind of the story. Today is the first chance we've had to be alone to talk.

"I've been better," I say, shaking off the melancholy clinging to me.

"Are you having nightmares?"

I don't bother hiding the truth, she knows me too well.

"I am, but they've changed.

"What do you mean? Changed how?"

"The person in my nightmare isn't a scared fifteen-year-old girl."

"Who is it?"

"It's me, now. I'm older and stronger and I fight back."

"So why are they nightmares, if you fight back?"

"Because he still wins. He still rapes me every time."

Raina rounds the breakfast bar and pulls me into her arms for a hug. The sudden contact forces me to let go of the tears I've been holding back for three days. She holds me tight as I fall apart, sobbing uncontrollably. The tears flow until all the fear, anger, frustration, and helplessness have washed away. And when the clouds of sorrow and pain have lifted, I feel almost normal again.

Leading me to the couch, Raina urges me to take a seat. She returns to the kitchen and dampens a paper towel. Taking a seat next to me, she cleans my face.

"Better," she says, but it's not a question. She knows as well as I do that only time will make this better.

"Thank you."

"What are friends for, if you can't actually cry on their shoulder?"

"Are you ready for lunch?" I ask, needing to move past the storm into the sunlight.

Standing, I walk to the breakfast bar and Raina follows me. We serve ourselves, before sitting down to enjoy our meal. We stay clear of any depressing topics, choosing only to talk about our next social event. With only two days left before Katelyn's art gallery opening, Raina wants to do some shopping.

"I need shoes," she says. "Because a girl can never have too many pairs of shoes."

That makes me laugh. It's a genuine laugh and it feels good.

"I think I need shoes too."

"Good, I'll pick you up tomorrow for lunch and we'll spend the afternoon shopping."

"A little retail therapy. I can handle that."

"Okay, we have a date then."

Raina helps me with the dishes before I walk her to the elevator.

"I'll see you tomorrow," she says as the elevator door closes between us.

I feel a little lighter entering the penthouse. It feels like a weight has been lifted off my shoulders. There is just one more thing I need to do before I'm totally free from the shame of my past. Tell Lucian the whole truth.

Just as he promised, Lucian arrives home at 6:30. The moment he enters the foyer, my body responds to his proximity. He joins me in the kitchen. Standing behind me, Lucian's powerful arms encircle me. I close my eyes, breathing him in.

"I missed you today," Lucian says, his lips at my neck, brushing against my skin.

He presses one hand to my stomach, holding me closer to him. The sensual embrace makes me achingly aware of his hunger. He nibbles at my ear, telling me that food is not what he's craving. Desire burns through me like a heatwave, searing my skin.

I grab the hand pressing against my stomach, guiding it under my skirt to my center.

"Rose Petal." His husky voice is filled with need. It has been two days since we've made love. Two days of quick kisses and polite conversation; two days of emptiness.

His finger circles my clit and I whimper. "Wider," he groans.

I spread my legs for him, welcoming his exploration. Two fingers enter me, sliding in and out. My heart pounds in my chest, and my pussy clenches around his fingers. Trembling uncontrollably, my knees become weak. Lucian's protective arms hold me tighter. My head falls against his chest, and I roll my hips. Grinding my ass against the stiffness of his erection, begging for more. With Lucian, I always want more.

"Come for me my rose petal." His fingers delve deeper, and I grind my hips, racing toward the release I so desperately need.

My orgasm comes in waves, like a rushing tide, wiping me out. I fall over the edge in Lucian's arms, knowing he will always be there to tether me.

When I'm breathing normally again and able to stand on my own two feet, Lucian frees me from his embrace.

"Are you okay?" he asks, turning me to face him.

"I'm fine," I say, but it's a lie. I've been stressing all afternoon, worrying how my secret will affect our relationship.

He nods, a frown marring his handsome face. "How was lunch with Raina?"

"It was good. We're meeting for lunch again tomorrow."

"But something is bothering you."

"Yes," I say, my throat chokes with shame.

"Do you want to tell me about it?"

I take Lucian by the hand and lead him to the couch. With my head bowed, I sit facing him. He waits patiently for me to speak. I pull away when Lucian reach for my hand.

"You may not want to touch me once you hear what I have to say."

His body becomes rigid, and he leans back like he's bracing himself for an assault.

"Are you leaving me? Did you cheat on me?" The words come out as if it pained him to say them.

"Oh, god no," I say, rushing forward and kneeling at his side. "But I've lied to you and kept secrets from you."

Lucian lifts my chin, so we are eye to eye. "What have you lied about and what secrets have you kept?"

I clear my throat and begin.

"Ten years ago, the week before you found me and took me to the hospital was the lowest point of my life. And that shame still haunts me. It was apparent right away that something was different from all the nights before."

"What do you mean, different?" Lucian asks.

"Please let me get through this."

A single tear rolls down my cheek and Lucian wipes it away.

"Alright."

"When he entered the room, he greeted me with gentle words, complimenting me. Whereas before he was always cruel and abusive. When he climbed onto the bed with me, he didn't force his way into my body. He touched me tenderly, like a lover would. And my body responded, betraying me. I didn't want it. I tried to fight, to resist his touch. But I failed. I couldn't stop him. I couldn't stop myself. I couldn't stop the orgasm. My first. Later, when he raped me, there was no pain like all the other times he'd raped me. When it was over, all I felt was a sickening shame that caused me to become ill. I wanted him to punish me, and he did. Ten lashes with a thick leather belt across my ass. I remained silent, refusing to cry. Instead, I taunted him with my laughter, infuriating him more. In that moment, I wanted to die. He had made me enjoy it, after everything he had done to me. I was so ashamed. And I believed it meant I must have wanted it somehow. After that night I intentionally provoked him, welcoming the punishment. Because I thought I deserved it."

I take a breath, opening the floodgates of tears I've been keeping at bay. Lucian pulls me onto his lap, holding me to his chest. And for the second time today, cleansing tears wash away the clouds. Lucian strokes my back, soothing me as he had ten years ago. We have come full circle, with no more lies and secrets between us. With all that's happened this week, I hope we can now put the past fully behind us and truly start to heal.

When Lucian finally speaks, his voice is loving, and his words are comforting.

"You have nothing to be ashamed of. None of what happened to you was your fault or your choice. What they did to you is their shame, not yours. It doesn't belong to you so don't take it on. Let the guilt and shame go, Sweetness. You're better than them and they can't have any part of you."

"I never meant to lie to you," I say, "it was just so hard to admit that to anyone."

"It wasn't a lie. You felt guilty for something that wasn't your fault. And I understand that."

I sigh, knowing he speaks the truth. Lucian has had to deal with his own guilt in the past and again more recently.

"How was the appointment with Dr. Reynolds?" I ask.

"It was a good start. I'm seeing her again next week."

"Do you think we should try couples' therapy?"

"Do you think we need it, as a couple?" he queries.

"No," I answer quickly because it's the one thing I'm sure of beyond a doubt. Together, Lucian and I work like nothing else in my life ever has. "No," I repeat. "Our bond has always been the one constant I can depend on. Even before I knew you, I trusted it. And now that I'm in love with you it's perfect."

"I..." Lucian's iPhone ringing stops him from finishing his sentence.

"Thorne," he says into the device. He listens for a moment, then says, "Avery's here with me. I'm putting you on speaker."

"What is it?" I whisper.

"Go ahead, Jake, we're listening."

"Clayton Fields is trying to get a plea deal in exchange for testifying against Samantha. Now that he knows that Samantha killed Camille, he's worried about his own skin."

"What are they charging him with?" Lucian asks.

"Right now, he's facing kidnapping, assault, and stalking charges. But that could change if he provides any useful information against Samantha."

"Samantha's parents arrived last night. They've hired a defense attorney for her."

"Yeah, I know. It's Danica Drake," Jake says.

"What can you tell me about her?"

"She graduated top of her class at Princeton. She's never lost a case and she's considered the best defense attorney is Chicago. Jake pauses before asking, "Are you attending Samantha's arraignment tomorrow?"

"No, I don't want another run in with the Davies'. They stopped by Thorne Tower today to see me. Pleaded with me for leniency for Samantha. Said they couldn't bear to lose another child."

I gasp, the insensitivity of his ex-in-laws shocking me. My reaction draws Lucian's attention. He strokes my cheek and pulls me closer.

"What the fuck!" Jake blurts out. "They can't be serious."

"I can assure you they are. They even went as far as to blame me. Accusing me of leading Samantha on and using her after Camille's death."

"I do have some good news for you," Jake offers. "The civil suit has been dismissed and you're officially no longer a person of interest in the deaths of Cam and Ian."

"It was never about the money for Samantha. She was obsessed with trying to gain something from me I could never give. Not then and certainly not now. My heart was never hers to bargain with."

After a bit of small talk, Jake says goodnight.

"Why didn't you tell me the Davies' stopped by the office to see you?" I ask after the call ends.

"I was going to, but we had other matters to discuss."

"Are you okay? It had to be upsetting to be attacked like that."

"I am, and it was. Luckily it happened before my appointment with Dr. Reynolds. I was able to get quite a bit off my chest during our session."

"Let's keep doing this. Sharing everything," I clarify.

"Always, Miss West."

"I love you, Mr. Thorne."

Lucian's mouth descends on mine, devouring my lips. His hand fists my hair, and he takes what he needs from me. The kiss seems to go on forever. I'm lost in his aggressive claiming. Intoxicated by his seductive groans and his possessive hold. Without warning, he lifts me, carrying me to our bedroom.

"I would have turned the world upside down to find you. Nothing will ever keep me away from you," Lucian says, laying me down on the bed.

He undresses me, peeling away each layer until I'm naked before him.

"I want to possess you in every way," he groans. "I want to fill you up and make you scream my name."

Lucian's fingers glide over my skin, slowly, deliberately, blazing a trail to my soaking wet center. He observes as my body reacts to his touch, arching and writhing as goosebumps mark the path he has taken.

"Including here." His finger caresses the pucker of my asshole.

"Yes," I say. "I trust you completely. I want to be yours in every possible way."

He smiles. "Are you sure?"

"Absolutely. I want everything with you."

"What's your safe word, Avery?"

"Lighthouse."

"Use it if you need to."

"I will."

Lucian stands, removing his clothes until he's completely naked before me. He climbs onto the bed. Crawling between my legs, he spreads them wide. My hips buck forward when his tongue flicks my clit.

"So responsive," he moans.

Lucian's head drops between my thighs, licking and teasing, nipping and sucking, tasting and devouring. And when I'm convinced, I can't handle anymore, he inserts two fingers in my throbbing wet center. I detonate on contact, clenching tightly around his fingers.

I have barely recovered when he orders me to get on my hands and knees. His fingers, slick with my essence, press against my ass. I open for him, eager to receive him. I feel the pucker of my ass blossoming like a flower. Gripping my hips, Lucian pulls me to him, pressing a kiss to the back of my neck. He pushes one finger in, stretching me gently and slowly before adding a second and third finger. He pulls his finger out and pushes them back in, finger fucking my ass harder and faster. He stops, pulling out as I'm about to shatter.

Lucian positions his dick against my asshole and pushes forward slowly. His entry is made easy by the two orgasms and the stretching with his fingers. My body accepts him, drawing him in, turning the pain into mind-numbing pleasure. His teeth graze my neck and I tremble in his arms. I'm sitting on his lap, his cock buried deep in my ass, and all I want is to kiss him. Angling my body, I turn to face him. Our eyes lock, and my heart swells, overjoyed by the love I see in his heated gaze. I cover his mouth with mine, taking what I need.

Lucian fills me completely. His tongue in my mouth, his cock in my ass, and his fingers in my pussy. An erotic possession, like nothing I have ever experienced. He thrusts into me over and over, growling my name. He's close, and so am I. His thumb strokes my clit, in sync with his cock penetrating my ass. The sensation overwhelms me.

"Lucian!" I scream, through an orgasm that shatters my soul, healing it at the same time.

He follows me over the edge, growling incoherently. Words of love and devotion. His body shudders, filling me with his seed. Clenching my ass, I milk him.

"Fuck," he groans in my ear when he's able to speak again. "Do you have any idea how much I fucking love you?"

"As much as I fucking love you." I say, offering him my mouth.

"Shower with me?" Lucian asks, after breaking the kiss.

Climbing out of bed, we make our way to the bathroom and step into the shower. We make love two more times. And three hours after he walked into the kitchen, Lucian was finally ready for dinner.

Chapter 20
Lucian

I AM ALONE IN BED, when I awake, missing the feel of Avery's body pillowing mine. She has slept peacefully the past two nights cradled in my arms. My sleep is improving as well. I'm sure that has everything to do with Avery. She has been ravenous with my body, taking what she wants from me. But I can't complain. My rose petal seems to have no limits when it comes to sharing her body with me. We fall into an exhausted sleep, only to wake craving more.

Climbing out of bed, I pull on my pajama bottoms and go in search of Avery. My nose and cock lead the way. The smell of freshly brewed coffee tells me she's in the kitchen. My cock arrowing towards her as I get closer confirms it. I watch her moving about the kitchen, placing items on a tray.

Avery pauses briefly, smiling, before saying, "I wanted to surprise you with naked breakfast in bed." Raising her head, she meets my gaze.

"Good morning, beautiful," I say, approaching the breakfast bar.

She meets me halfway, planting a kiss on my lips.

"Good morning," she says. The hint of cinnamon on her breath warms my face.

"We've had breakfast in bed naked. It's the best part of Saturday mornings."

"I know. But you usually serve me breakfast. I wanted to do the same for you," she pouts.

"You're so sexy when you're pouting," I tease.

"I don't pout."

"And you're even sexier when you're pouting about not pouting."

I wrap my arms around her, pulling her close. When my hands slide down to cup her ass, she has managed to surprise me after all. Her backside is gloriously bare. The apron she's wearing is all she's wearing. Craving the heat from a spanking, my palms twitch against her round ass.

"Surprise," she whispers, wiggling her ass.

My naughty girl tempts me in the most delectable ways. And I love every mouthwatering moment.

"There's more," she continues.

She steps back, releasing herself from my hold. I watch her reach behind her back, untying the apron. First from around her waist and then her neck. The apron falls to the floor. My beautiful rose petal stands naked before me, revealing another surprise. Her brown nipples are in clamps and are pebble hard.

"Fuck," I groan

"We'll get to that," she teases, as she turns her back to me.

She pads barefoot to the kitchen. I stare, mesmerized by her luscious ass.

"Are you coming? Would you like something to eat?" she says over her shoulder.

Avery's double entendre are intentional. She wants to entice me. And she wants me on her terms. The dominant in me rarely yields control. But the submissive in her needs to know that I won't lose control. Even when she pushes me beyond my limits.

"Is this a test?" I ask, following her. "Making me wait for what's already mine."

"If it's already yours, what's the harm in savoring the feast?"

"If?" I question.

"Since it's already yours." She amends.

Standing behind her, I whisper against her ear. "There's no harm in savoring a meal. But I should warn you, the longer I wait, the hungrier I tend to get." Avery lets out a soft moan when I lick her earlobe.

"Fuck the waiting," she says, turning to face me. Avery wrap her arms around my neck. I lift her, and with quick strides I carry her to the couch. Laying her down, I climb between her legs. Her hands fist my hair, pulling my head down to her. I kiss her lips intending to savor her.

However, Avery has other plans, reminding me that this is still on her terms. Avery moans into my mouth, deepening our kiss. The kiss is voracious, her mouth claiming mine with an insatiable hunger.

I fucking love this woman.

"Tell me that you love me. Tell me that you're mine," she murmurs against my lips. The combination of cinnamon and her natural sweetness intoxicates me.

"I do. I am."

"Say the words, Lucian," she pleas.

"I. Love. You." I enunciate each word. "I love you in a way I never felt with anyone. I love you with every bit of my soul. I'd give up everything if it meant I could be with you and keep you safe. I'm yours. Always."

"My life would be incomplete without you."

"You'll never be without me."

My mouth descends upon hers in a kiss I hope is reassuring. I have no idea where the doubt has suddenly come from. The one thing I know for sure is that Avery and I are meant to be. We have a bond that's always and forever. Whatever assurances she needs, I will give.

Breaking the kiss, she pants, "Make love to me, Lucian."

Pushing my pajama bottoms down past my hips, Avery frees my cock. She spreads her legs wider, and I fist my cock, guiding it into her wet heat. Avery clenches around me, drawing me in. She moans when I bottom out, filling her utterly. I hold still for a moment, pressing my face into the crook of her neck. Withdrawing slowly from her body, I slide back into her, sinking my long shaft deep. Avery's fingers glide through my hair, and she whispers in my ear.

"My feelings for you are too intense and I can't turn off how it makes me feel."

"Don't ever fucking turn it off," I growl, my lips brushing against her neck.

Rolling my hips, I pick up the pace, burying myself deep, getting lost in her. Our breathing ramps up as the rising passion between us builds. I drop my head, teasing her clamped nipples with my tongue. Increasing the pressure, Avery moans, arching into me.

"Fuck," I groan. The sound is almost primal. "You were made for me, Avery."

"You're the only man for me, Lucian," she pants breathlessly.

Hooking one leg over my shoulder, a ferocious growl escapes my throat as I plunge deeper. I rock into her body, grinding hard and fast. Avery tightens around me, chasing her release. When she's close, I remove the nipple clamps and whisper, "You'll always be mine. Just as surely as I'm forever yours."

My words push her over the edge, screaming my name. Her orgasm is so intense, tears roll down her cheeks. I hold her close, when my own release shudders my body, filling her with my seed. Marking her as mine.

Avery and I take a quick shower before we finally have naked breakfast.

• • • •

A FEW HOURS LATER WE'RE in the back of the limo heading to SoHo. We've volunteered to help Katelyn set-up for her art gallery opening tonight.

When we arrive, the sign says closed, but the door is unlocked. When Avery and I enter Katelyn Thorne Fine Art Gallery, I glance around. Smiling at my sister's accomplishment, I can't hide how proud I am of her. There's still a lot of preparation to be done before the opening.

The walls are stark white to showcase the artwork. And that's why I'm here, to hang the art I've loaned Katelyn for her gallery's first exhibition.

"Where are you going to hang your paintings?" Avery asks.

I look around for the location of the Lucian Thorne Art Collection. I've agreed to loan five pieces from my private collection, for one year. Katelyn wants to showcase them to attract an upscale clientele to her gallery. People who are not only lovers of art, but who also buy art.

Touring the gallery, Avery and I get a sneak peek at some of the exhibits. We turn a corner and find ourselves at the back of the gallery. And ahead of us are Marcus and Katelyn, who seem oblivious of our presence. When Marcus strokes Katelyn's cheek and says, "I'm so proud of you Allikat," I feel like I'm intruding on an intimate moment. Especially, when he plants a kiss on Katelyn's lips.

Taking Avery by the hand, I turn back.

"Allikat?" Avery questions.

"Katelyn didn't like her name growing up. She made everyone call her Allie. Everyone, except Marcus."

"Isn't she named after your grandmother, Kathleen?"

"Yes. But she also didn't want to be called Kat or Kate like our grandmother. So, we all agreed to call her Allie, short for Alyssa, her middle name."

"Are you upset by what we saw? Would it bother you if your best friend and sister got together?"

"Hell no. I'm just surprised it's taking them so long. They've been crazy about each other since Marcus, Jake, and I were in high school."

"It's obvious, whenever they're in the same room together they can't take their eyes off each other."

"We all know Marcus has feelings for Katelyn. He's had it bad for a long time. But nothing has ever come from it. They've only ever been friends."

"If it's obvious to everyone, why aren't they together?"

"I don't know what's keeping them apart now. But as kids, I respected that he didn't try to date her back then. My best friend dating my kid sister would have fucked up our friendship. We were all he had, and he needed all of us. Now that we're all adults, I can't think of any reason why they aren't together."

"Is Katelyn dating anyone?"

"She was seeing some guy when she was living in Los Angeles. But that was over three years ago."

"Maybe there's hope for them now that they're in the same state and working together."

"I love your optimism."

"I just want everyone to be as happy as we are."

"Are you happy, Sweetness?" I probe.

"Blissfully so."

I pull her into my arms, kissing her passionately. When we hear someone clearing their throat. My sister, no doubt. Reluctantly, we break the kiss.

"Did you come to help or to make out with your girlfriend?" Katelyn teases.

"A little of both," I say, giving Avery a quick peck on the lips before letting her go.

Katelyn greets us when she has our full attention.

"You just missed Marcus. He was here putting the finishing touches on his exhibit," Katelyn says. "I'll show you where I want your collection." Leading the way, Avery and I follow my sister.

"The gallery looks great," Avery says.

"Do you really think so?" Katelyn questions.

"I do," Avery assures.

"I've been freaking out all morning, worrying I might have forgotten something," Katelyn confesses.

"You have nothing to worry about. But if it makes you feel better, I can go over your checklist. A second set of eyes never hurts."

Katelyn stops in her tracks, grabs Avery's hand, and says, "You would do that for me?"

"We're here to help with whatever you need," Avery vows.

"I love you." Katelyn squeals with delight, giving Avery a quick hug.

I know the feeling.

Over the next several hours, the three of us tackle Katelyn's list. Everything from the caterers, hanging art, sweeping, and some light dusting.

When we're done, I have a chance to view Marcus's paintings. I know my best friend has talent, but the pieces he's showcasing are exceptional. Three in all. The paintings depict a faceless woman undressing for her lover, whose reflection is seen in a mirror. Each painting reveals more than the one before. The woman is completely naked in the third painting, revealing only her backside. The paintings are erotically sensual, yet completely innocent.

"They're good, aren't they?" Katelyn says, standing beside me.

"Extremely good," I agree. "You should have no problem selling these."

"They aren't for sale."

'Isn't the whole point of an art gallery to sell the paintings?"

She chuckles. "Your collection isn't for sale," she reminds me. "Besides, all his other work is for sale."

"I saw you and Marcus together earlier. You look quite friendly."

"Is there a question in there somewhere, big brother?"

"Is there something going on between you two?"

Katelyn takes a deep breath and releases it before saying, "What if there were something between us. Would you be okay with that?"

"Why wouldn't I be? I can see how much you've always cared about him."

"I more than care about him, Lucian."

I nod, understanding the depths of her feelings. What I don't understand is why she has never done anything about it.

"Then why aren't you with him?"

"He doesn't want me." Her voice cracks. "He says family is too important for him to risk. That the cost is too high."

I wrap my arm around Katelyn's shoulders, comforting her as best I can. When she begins to tremble with silent sobs, I share my observations.

"I have thought for a long time that Marcus is in love with you. When you walk into a room, he can't take his eyes off you. Even when he's trying to ignore you, it's impossible for him. I don't know why he's keeping his distance. But don't let him use it as an excuse for not being with you. Because it's the worst kept secret. We all know he's crazy about you."

That makes her laugh. Turning to face me her big brown eyes are blurry with her tears.

"Thank you," she sniffles.

"For what?"

"For reminding me that Thornes never give up. And Marcus is worth fighting for."

"Anytime. That's what big brothers are for."

Avery rejoins us, just as Katelyn finish wiping away her tears. We make our way to the front door. Katelyn thanks us again for our help. Franklin is at the curb waiting when Avery and I leave the gallery.

Katelyn locks the door behind us, watching as the limo pulls away.

"Is Katelyn alright?" Avery asks once we're underway.

My rose petal doesn't miss a thing. Always so observant.

"She'll be okay. She just needed to vent a little."

Avery accepts my answer, snuggling into my side. My thoughts turn to Marcus and how he's denying his true feelings for my sister. And then I look at Avery and I can't imagine not telling her everyday how much I love her. How much she means to me. I suppose every love story is different and theirs will unfold in due time.

• • • •

AVERY AND I ARE DRESSED and ready to leave for the gallery opening, when she says, "Help me with this please." Her diamond choker dangles between her fingers.

The sight of my collar makes me hard instantly. The last time she wore it was the day she was taken. Franklin found it tuck between the seats of her BMW. The fact that she had left it behind told me it wasn't voluntary. She allows me to collar her, and she waits for me to remove it. When she wears it, she's totally submissive, and totally fucking sexy.

"Are you sure?" I ask.

"I'm your submissive tonight, Sir."

I take the necklace from Avery's hand, my gaze fixed on hers.

"Turn around," I command

She spins, showing me her back. I can't help leaning down and kissing her collarbone. Placing my collar around her neck, I pull her to me. She moans softly when she feels my hard-bulging cock pressing against her back.

"I'm tempted to make you sweaty before we leave. Fill you with my seed and let it soak your panties," I whisper in her ear.

"Yes, please." Her voice is breathy and needy, the sound is addictive.

"Soon, Rose Petal. I promise."

Reluctantly, I step away from her, for my own benefit. The need to lay her bare and fuck her senseless grows with every breath I take.

When we finally arrive at the gallery, the place is packed. Katelyn's guest list is impressive. She has invited everyone from politicians to starving artists, whose works are on display tonight. Our brother Daniel is here as well. He has recently come out, announcing during a press conference that he's gay. He didn't disclose that he was currently in a relationship. However, tonight marks the first public appearance with his partner, Christopher Adams.

I can't say that my brother being gay has surprised me. It has only made some things clearer. When he confessed to his affair with Camille he also begged for forgiveness, saying he never set out to use Camille or betray me. He also said, "Denying who I am, has come at a cost. I've hurt so many people." At the time, the statement didn't make since. Now that I see him, see how happy he is with Chris, I realize he was using Camille to deny his sexuality. Maybe not from the public, but from himself. He confided to me once that he preferred men but was also attracted to women. However, he was in a state of drunkenness at the time. I know that my brother regrets his actions with my deceased wife. Forgiving them wasn't easy but letting go of the pain of their betrayal has led me to Avery. Although Camille will always be a part of my life. Avery is my life.

I keep Avery close as we make our way through the crowd in search of the hostess for this event. When we find her, Katelyn is surrounded by several art enthusiasts expressing interest in the same painting. If I had to guess, I'd say the young woman shying away from all the attention is the artist. Katelyn acknowledges our arrival with a smile and a nod, but otherwise continues with her conversation.

The next forty-five minutes is a rapid parade of introductions. I take the time to personally thank my colleagues for supporting my sister. In the process, most of them meet Avery. She won't remember their names, and it's not important. However, it is important that they remember her and how much she means to me.

Servers move through the crowd of art patrons carrying trays of appetizers and champagne. I won't indulge in any alcohol tonight. The woman at my side already has my head spinning. I refuse to dull my senses when I intend to enjoy the pleasures she offers. My cock twitches in anticipation.

"Have you seen the Morgan Dare exhibit?" Raina whispers to Avery, when she joins us, along with Jake and Marcus.

"Not yet," Avery answers, "But I intend to see everything."

"Jake and I just left it and I think I need to change my damn panties." This woman is the worst at whispering. But I'm grateful for the information.

I tune the women out, greeting my two best friends.

"Congratulations!" I say, shaking Marcus's hand. "I saw that two of your paintings have already been sold." Jake also congratulates him.

"There's a lot of talent here tonight your sister included. I just got lucky, and my livelihood doesn't depend on a sale tonight. Some of the artists here would never have such a large audience for their work if it wasn't for Katelyn. She's the one that should be congratulated for putting all this together," Marcus says. "But thanks, I appreciate it."

Jake gives me a knowing look, because it seems Marcus can't help sharing his accomplishments with Katelyn, giving her most of the credit.

Before I can say anything, Jake blurts out. "Why aren't you with Katelyn? It's obvious you've got it bad for her."

Embarrassed, Marcus stumbles over his words. The man who speaks eloquently and is never at a loss for words is dumbstruck. When he finds the words, he says, "Katelyn is like my sister."

Jake laughs. "Bull shit," he says. "I don't look at my sister the way you look at Katelyn."

"No one should look at your sister that way," I retort. "She's ten." Laughter breaks out and we draw attention from onlookers.

"You know what I mean, smart ass." Jake grins.

"I do," Marcus says, all traces of his laughter gone. "But Katelyn is my family. End of story."

Respecting Marcus's wish, Jake changes the subject.

The five of us are viewing the work of a local sculptor, when Katelyn announces that the performance art portion of tonight's exhibition is about to begin. Everyone gathers around the area Katelyn has corded off, waiting for the performer.

A young Caucasian man takes to the stage and begins dancing to hip hop music, to a song I'm not familiar with. He dances around an unmoving statue, which is obviously a female dancer. The statue begins to stretch as if waking from a long sleep. The African American female dancer, a ballerina, moves in sync with the hip-hop dancer. The dance is beautiful and entertaining. The audience applauds, cheering loudly when the performance is over.

"Did you like it?" Avery asks.

"I enjoyed the performance, but I didn't recognize the song."

"The Canvas, by SiR," Avery says. "It fits perfectly, bringing the elements of the art exhibition together."

"Katelyn has always been able to find symbolism in art and music," I attest.

Leading Avery away from our friends, I make my way to the exhibit I've wanted her to see all night. We're standing before a showcase of photographs, when Avery lets out a small gasp followed by a soft moan. Her reaction is perfect. The crowd has thinned out and we're mostly secluded in the small alcove. I pull her directly in front of me, my cock pressing against her back. She stares at the collection of twelve erotically charged black and white photos depicting a different BDSM scene. The photographer has a true artist's eye. The images are provocative and sexy without being pornographic.

"The collection is called The Art of Submission," I whisper in Avery's ear.

She doesn't speak, but her breathing hitches when my lips brush against the shell of her ear.

In the first photo, the model is wearing a blindfold and her hands are suspended above her head, bound to a St. Andrew's Cross.

We move onto the next few photos and Avery barely has a reaction. When we reach the fifth photograph in the series, Avery steps closer examining it. The photo is titled, Kinbaku-bi.

"It's Japanese bondage. The word kinbaku-bi literally means, the beauty of tight binding," I explain. "How does it make you feel?"

"The rope work is beautiful," Avery says, her voice husky with need.

"It is. But how does it make you feel?" I repeat.

Avery clears her throat. "Frightened and aroused. But mostly aroused."

"What about it arouses you?"

The image is visually artistic, exuding eroticism and sexuality. The connection between the model and the photographer is evident. The trust even more so.

"She's bound with the rope, totally helpless. But the expression on her face conveys bliss and freedom."

"The ropes are meant to restrain, but the placement is meant solely for pleasure."

I stand behind her, wrapping my arm around her. Placing my hand flat against her stomach, I hold her close. She moans, gently twirling her hips.

"Does it make you wet knowing that I'm hard for you? That I'm aching for you?"

"Yes, Sir. It does."

"I've imagined taking you in one of the alcoves. Touching you, making you wetter. Stroking your clit slowly, feeling it swell beneath my fingers." I grind my hips slowly against her back, letting her feel how hard I am for her.

"Why don't you, Sir?" Her words are more a plea than a question.

"I can smell your arousal and I want to taste it. I crave it. I can never get enough of its sweetness. But if I do what I want, I won't be able to stop. I'm too desperate to be inside you."

"What if I don't want you to stop, Sir?"

"Don't tempt me, Rose Petal," I growl, my voice barely recognizable.

Avery turns to face me. Her beautiful hazel eyes are dark with lust and mischief. She wraps her arms around my neck and whispers against my lips. "Which one is your favorite?"

My beautiful temptress covers my mouth with hers before I can respond. But the image has been burnt into my brain the moment I saw it. I imagine the model is Avery. She's laid bare on my bed, her hands bound above her head, her legs spread wide with a spreader bar. And a red silk scarf blindfolds her. Her lips are slightly parted, waiting for me. The image in my head becomes more vivid with each twirl of her tongue against mine.

"Take me home." Her words spill into my mouth. "You promised to make me sweaty. To fill me with your seed," she moans.

"I also promised to soak your panties."

"I'm dripping wet for you, Sir."

"Then I think it's time I kept the rest of my promises."

Avery and I say a hasty goodnight to our family and friends. We're practically running out the door when we bump into a man leaving at the same time.

"Excuse us," Avery giggles, pulling me out the door with her.

Franklin has the back-passenger door of the limo open when we reach the curb. Avery climbs in and I follow her eagerly. The limo pulls into traffic, and I pull Avery into my arms. We make out in the back of the limo like teenagers on prom night. We didn't realize the limo had come to a stop until Franklin taps on the window.

We take the elevator alone to the penthouse. The air between us is sexually charged and I can't keep my hands off her. I grab her, my body pinning hers to the wall. Lifting her leg, she wraps it around my back. My body trembles with need, seeking release. Her mouth claims mine, kissing me roughly. My breathing is hard, and she takes my breath away. She breaks the kiss and whispers, "Before the night is through I wanna do bad things with you." The lyrics to Jace Everett's Bad Things make Avery wet and needy every time she hears our ringtone. The lyrics also affect me but hearing them in Avery's voice has me desperate to lose myself in her. The elevator door slides open, and I lift Avery off her feet, carrying her into the foyer. Avery's iPhone beeps indicating an incoming text.

"I should get that. It could be important," she pants.

"Leave it until tomorrow," I command gently. "Whoever it is can wait until tomorrow. Because tonight I wanna do bad things with you."

• • • •

Thank You

I WANT TO THANK YOU for reading Undeniable Bond. I hope you enjoy getting to know Lucian and Avery as much as I did. Their story will continue in Inseparable Bond, the third book in the Bonded Series.

If you haven't done so already, please take the time to review my book. It is the best way for readers to find lesser-known authors. And if you have, thank you so much, I truly appreciate your support.

• • • •

Happy Reading and Happy Endings!

About the Author

Reese Spenser is both author and a ravenous reader of romance. She began her career as a contemporary romance author with her debut novel Tainted Bond. However, she has always been fascinated with the supernatural. It was her weakness for vampires and shifters, and her addiction to mythology and fairytales, that led her to begin writing paranormal romance. When she's not busy writing, she enjoys spending time with family and friends and spoiling her grandchildren.

Read more at reesespenser.com.

www.ingramcontent.com/pod-product-compliance
Lightning Source LLC
LaVergne TN
LVHW091132080826
845145LV00008B/2121
9781393329985